LAST ONE STANDING

THE BIGGER YOU ARE, THE HARDER YOU FALL.

MARIA FRANKLAND

AUTONOMY
PRESS

First published by Autonomy Press 2024

Copyright © 2024 by Maria Frankland

This novel is entirely a work of fiction. The names, characters and incidents portrayed in it are the work of the author's imagination. Any resemblance to actual persons, living or dead, events or localities is entirely coincidental.

Maria Frankland asserts the moral right to be identified as the author of this work.

First edition

Cover Design by David Grogan www.headdesign.co.uk

For Michael – thanks for our amazing first sunshine holiday in Bodrum. No work was permitted... (other than the notes for this book!!)

JOIN MY 'KEEP IN TOUCH' LIST

If you'd like to be kept in the loop about new books and special offers, join my 'keep in touch list' here or by visiting <u>www.mariafrankland.co.uk</u>

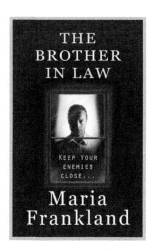

PROLOGUE

I FEEL ALMOST invincible out here. As if nothing and nobody can touch me. I can nearly forget the *real* reason I've ended up in this place, this absolute *paradise*. I've certainly never swum in warmer waters which are so clear, I'm almost at one with the fish around me.

I slick my fringe, heavy with salt, back from my forehead and enjoy the heat of the morning sun on my face. I power on, continuing to relish this unexpected freedom and the opportunity to clear my head. It's been a complete mess lately with everything that's happened. And just as it was starting to settle, life's been upended again.

The hum of an approaching speedboat cuts into my peace. It's a surprise to see anyone else this early in the morning. With a bit of luck, it will just spin around and head back out again. I certainly haven't got the energy to make pointless small talk this morning if it docks here. That's if they even speak any English.

But, if anything, the speedboat is getting faster, slicing through the turquoise waves like a knife through butter. Its roar sets my teeth on edge as I glance back to where I left my things. Perhaps I'd be best to swim back in that direction.

But the speedboat also alters its course, bouncing closer and closer. And if I didn't know better, I'd say it was heading straight towards me.

Has its driver even noticed me out here?

I pause, tread water and wave my arms in the air but still, it keeps coming. I have to get out of the way.

Now.

My arms flail through the now choppier waters – it's like swimming through treacle. And I'm no longer in any doubt – that speedboat *is* coming at me.

There's a split second in which the driver and I lock eyes while I make one last attempt to get out of the way. But the roar of the speedboat vibrates through me as a searing pain shoots through my shoulder. I'm on my back, my eyes wide open. Somehow I'm still floating on the surface. I'm still here. I'm alive.

I spit the salty water, or could it be blood, from my mouth. As I squint at the rear of the speedboat, I realise I've got another chance to get away. But it's turning around. As it spins in the waves, I gasp. It's heading right back at me.

This was meant to happen. And this time I'm done for.

PART I

DEBRA

1

DEBRA

'GET OFF ME!' I squeeze a sharp exhale of breath from my lungs as I sit bolt upright in bed, engulfed by panic as it takes a moment or two to register where I am. It's OK. I'm safe.

I have the same dream most nights. I'm standing in front of Bryn's coffin, head bowed, waiting for the final curtain to draw around him, when he suddenly springs from his coffin and grabs me by the throat, just like he did when he was trying to prevent me from leaving him on New Year's Eve.

I rub at my throat as I try to get my breath in. I'm perfectly safe, after all, my husband of nearly twenty-five years has been dead for just over four months. There's nothing he can do or say to hurt me anymore. His funeral is well and truly in the rearview mirror and thankfully, I haven't heard anything else from my daughter's ex, Carl or his turncoat mother, Tina. For me, their presence *together* at Bryn's funeral had taken my attention away from everything else that should have mattered. Like supporting my children.

'So the two of you *know* each other?' I'd marched straight over to Carl and Tina the moment I got out of the crematorium. Dressed from head to foot in black, like the rest of us, they looked like they belonged there. But they didn't – not one bit. I'd only met the woman *once*, when travelling home on New Year's Eve and thought I'd never see her again, least of all at my husband's funeral. And standing side by side with my daughter's toxic ex.

You could have blown me over when I found out who she was. If only I'd known I was spilling my guts to none other than *Carl's mother* on that train. As I wracked my brain to recall what I'd said about him, all I could recall was that it hadn't been very favourable.

'Small world.' She smiled as we uncovered our connection. 'I'm just here to give Carl some moral support today.' He looked as smug as she did.

'Moral support?' The plot thickened as I refrained from enquiring why on earth, *he'd* need moral support.

'As you know, Bryn meant a lot to Carl.' The look on her face said it all. What she was maybe thinking was *unlike he meant to you*.

'Carl, can you give us a minute please?' I should have been comforting my children and thanking people for coming but all that mattered in that moment was this grinning woman in front of me, the one I'd shared a couple of G&T's with, and far more besides. There was another reason she'd turned up that day and it was nothing to do with *moral support*.

'Sure.' Carl dug his hands into his pockets and sauntered over to where they'd started bringing the floral tributes out. He left his mother's side too easily and I could tell they must have planned everything.

'The stuff I told you on the train.' My words tumbled out in a bluster as I looked around to check no one was listening in. 'Obviously, I was just sounding off.' I laughed. 'I never dreamed in a million years that anything—' I couldn't finish my sentence. I didn't trust myself not to make things any worse.

'Of course you didn't, Debra.' As Tina reached for my arm, her use of my name sounded almost sinister. 'And I can imagine it's been a very tough time for you all.' Her face became serious.

'An absolute nightmare,' I agreed. 'Though after today—' I was about to talk about closure, hoping she'd take the hint and leave me alone.

'However,' she cut in, lowering her voice. 'I'm sure you'll want to see my son right for his involvement in all that went on, won't you?' She jerked her head in Carl's direction as he loitered near the doorway. If he tried collaring Hayley, I wouldn't be responsible for my actions. 'After what he was promised.'

'What do you mean?' Really, I knew *exactly* what she meant and the tone of her voice threatened consequences if I didn't agree with her.

'Carl was promised two grand up front, and a further three on completion.'

'That was between him and Bryn.' My voice was shaky. I'd struggled enough to hold it all together throughout the funeral service as it was.

'As his beneficiary—'

'I don't know what makes you think I have that sort of money lying around.' My voice was a hiss. 'I was left with nothing apart from the clothes I was standing up in when our pub burnt down.'

She seemed unmoved. 'I'm sure you wouldn't want to endure another inquest into Bryn's death, would you?'

'What?' I could hardly believe this was the same woman who'd listened and supposedly sympathised with my situation only months before. 'You can't... You wouldn't...'

'An inquest with *you* at the centre of it this time.' Her eyes were marble-hard.

I stared back at her as this new reality sank in. Tina and Carl had turned up at Bryn's funeral to blackmail me. They'd chosen a day when my defenses would be down and when I wouldn't want a scene in front of everyone. And if I didn't want my children to find out that their father *hadn't* died by suicide as they'd grown to accept, I'd have to find a way to get them off my back.

'There's no money left,' I mumbled. 'The man I told you about, the one I was supposed to be leaving with, Jay – he took it all.'

'Yeah, yeah.' She raised her eyes towards the clouds.

'And I don't know where he is.' I glanced over at Hayley who was looking at me quizzically as she stood with her brother and some relative of Bryn's. Carl had never introduced her to his mother so she'd have had no idea who I was so entrenched in conversation with. 'He'll have gone abroad somewhere. Look, I need to get back to my children.'

'I expect your insurance money will be landing any day though.' The smile that had returned to her face could barely mask the chill in her words. 'And Carl was promised a third of *that* as well.'

'But, but, I'm not sure—'

'Don't worry, Debra – we're not expecting you to conjure anything up *today*. But obviously, we *will* be back in touch.'

'How did you find me?' My words were almost a whisper. Her second use of my name had chilled my insides even further. I felt sure we'd parted ways at Leeds train station on first-name terms only.

'Oh, it was easy enough. I found you on Facebook,' she replied as I looked down, noticing how much her feet bulged from her ill-fitting and scuffed shoes. 'Anyway, we'll get going and leave you in peace – for now anyway.'

I should have been grateful they were leaving, grateful that I would have some breathing space and thinking time, but her words *for now* were so loaded with threat, I almost wanted to fall at her feet and beg her to leave me alone. I told her so much. *Everything, in* fact. Perhaps it was something to do with us sitting side by side on the train where no eye contact was made and I thought we'd never have to see one another again. She'd made all the right noises as I'd poured it all out and at the time we'd joked about how it was so much easier to talk to a complete stranger than a trusted friend. How could I have been so stupid to trust *anyone*?

'We just wanted to pay our respects to Bryn.' She pointed back towards the crematorium. Already the next family were at the main entrance, waiting with their loved one's coffin. I'd have bet my bottom dollar that they'd have died in more 'normal' circumstances and wouldn't be enduring this kind of dreadful aftermath. 'And to you, for the loss of your *husband*.'

The loaded way in which she said 'husband' set my teeth on edge even more. After all, we both knew that I'd come to the point where Bryn had been my husband in name only. And if I'd had my way, I'd have been sitting on some exotic beach with Jay by now with this place far behind me. Since spending so much time with my son and daughter over the last few months, I realise how selfish I was being. I regret my behaviour more than I've ever regretted anything but there's nothing I can do to undo things. All I can affect is the future.

'I really do need to—' My voice faded as I pointed towards where Lance was shaking hands with people as they continued to leave the building. A sea of black – most of them friends and regulars from The Dales Arms, our pub and former home. So badly damaged, it's now waiting for demolition.

'Who was *that*?' Hayley appeared at my side as Tina and Carl disappeared along the path to the main gate. There was an edge to her voice as though she could be jealous. 'She looks too old to be *with* Carl.'

'It's his mother,' I replied. 'She came with him for *moral support*, by all accounts.' I draw air quotes around the words.

'I didn't realise they were that close.' She scrunched her tissue up her sleeve. 'He never introduced us when we were together. Please tell me they're not going to be at the wake. I've managed to stay away from him so far today.'

'I don't think so.' My insides sagged at the realisation that I still had *that* to get through. Everyone talking about what a tragedy it had all been and what a senseless waste of life. All the time while giving me sidewards glances, no doubt blaming me for what had happened. After all, it was common knowledge that I'd been carrying on with Jay.

I thought I could move on after the funeral but Tina and Carl's little visit had ended any such hope. And even if I managed to raise the money to pay them off, how could I have ever been certain that they wouldn't come back for more? No, Bryn's little 'business' arrangement had landed me in a bigger hole than my husband was about to find himself in.

'Are you awake in there, Mum?' Hayley's outside my door. I can hardly believe I've been reduced to staying in the spare room of the house my daughter rents with her friend. But what else was I supposed to do after losing everything?

'Yeah.' I tug the covers up to my chin as if concealing the guilt which haunts me every time I look into her eyes. I don't know how I'll ever get over it. 'Come in, love.'

She pushes the door open and Sammy, our spaniel rushes in after her, bounding onto my bed with glee. If only I could have an ounce of her energy and exuberance. Hayley perches beside her on the edge of my bed, her hair unbrushed and wild. She passes me a letter. 'The postman's just been – I thought you'd want this.'

My stomach twists with nerves as I turn the thick envelope over in my hands, seeing from the franking that it's from the insurance company. Is its thickness a positive or negative sign?

'Open it then, Mum.'

My breath comes faster again as I finally tear into the paper with shaking hands. I've waited so long for this to arrive – the chance to clear some debts, pay Tina and Carl off once and for all, and then to be able to get back on my feet.

'Well?' Hayley tightens the cord of her dressing gown as I scan the contents of the covering letter. All I see are the phrases, 'will not pay out in the circumstances,' 'proven to be arson,' and 'right to appeal.'

'They're not paying out,' I tell her as the page flutters into my lap. I pinch the skin on the back of my hand as though wanting to wake myself from yet another bad dream.

'You're joking, aren't you? But what's the point of having insurance if—'

'It's because the fire was started deliberately.'

She gasps. 'But that wasn't *your* fault. *You* can't lose *everything* you've built up and worked for because of what *Dad* did?'

'I've already lost it all.' I throw the letter to one side, resisting the urge to tear it into tiny pieces. I can stare at the words all morning but nothing's going to change their decision.

'You must be able to appeal it?'

'I don't know if I could go through all that. Besides, it's unlikely to change much.' What I can't say to Hayley is that the police and the loss adjusters have already dug into our situation deeply enough. If I invite them to dig any deeper, who knows what they might find? Especially now that Tina and Carl are trying to extract their pound of flesh. 'Look it's fine, love. Other people have started again and I can start again too.' I attempt to load a conviction I'm not feeling into my words.

'At least you'll have something to come from Grandad's estate.' She rests her hand on my arm and looks at me with gentle eyes. This is Hayley all over. No matter what, she always sees the positives in things.

I close my eyes at this reminder. Losing Dad so soon after Bryn and the pub was just cruel. And because he lived for several years with Alzheimers before his death, it's been like losing him twice over.

'I can't imagine there'll be a great deal left over, Hayley. The care home and nursing fees have eaten into things more than I thought they might.' I don't add that once I've given her and Lance a bit of something and then paid to get Tina and Carl off my back, I'll be lucky to be left with anything much. Certainly not in the life-changing scheme of things anyway. I'm planning to offer Tina and

Carl the five grand she's already demanded. She looked so dowdy when I met her on the train, and two months ago at the funeral with her grey roots and chipped nails, that I'm certain she'll accept my offer. As for the insurance money, well I can't give them a third of what I haven't got. I'll show her the letter – even she should know you can't get blood out of a stone.

And if she doesn't accept my offer – well, who knows where things could end up.

2

DEBRA

EVERY DAY I do much the same thing. Stay in bed as late as possible, take a shower, sit on the doorstep with a coffee, take Sammy for a walk, mope around the house while Hayley and Gemma are out at work, and mindlessly scroll on social media. Well, it's not actually mindless at all. I'm scrolling with purpose.

I'm looking for Jay. Always, always, searching for Jay, in the hope that he might either reinstate his former profile, or set a new one up, thinking the dust's settled and that I'm getting on with my life. I'll never get over how he reeled me in and duped me so spectacularly – not just over the money he scammed me out of but how he also snatched away all the hopes I'd harboured for getting out there and living again. The excitement I'd felt had given me back my energy and purpose. But over the last few months, I've just felt as though I'm withering away. As I possibly deserve to.

Sighing in the silence, I glance up from my phone and catch sight of my reflection in the TV screen as the sun falls on it. My fiftieth birthday came and went without fanfare or incident. I certainly couldn't bring myself to 'celebrate' it in any way, even though the kids insisted on taking me out for a meal. All I could think about was the birthdays Bryn will never see again.

Right now, I feel every one of my fifty years and with the weight I've lost and the burden of stress after everything I've endured so far this year, I must look ten years older than I am. It's certainly been a very different few months to the time I was anticipating, swanning around hot beaches with a gorgeous, younger man on my arm.

Sammy sighs as she sleeps at my feet. My gaze falls on the photo Hayley has framed of herself and Lance with Dad in the middle of them. It was taken after his diagnosis but well before he declined enough to warrant moving to his care home. The kids have lost so much this year – their dad, their grandad, *and* the home they grew up in. They can't lose me as well, if Tina were to act on what she has on me. I *have* to somehow sort things out and pull myself back together – I owe it to my children.

My heart lurches as my phone beeps with a Messenger message.

> This is Tina again. I'm getting sick of you ignoring us. We've given you enough time to sort something out and need to know what you propose to do.

I feel like spitting at my phone screen. Speaking to her on that train is one of the worst mistakes I've ever made. Well, maybe the second biggest mistake. I still think she's full of hot air and won't *really* go to the police. After all, she risks incriminating her own son if she carries out her threats. One thing I know for certain is that if there's any chance of *me* being found out and punished, I'll be dragging her son right down with me.

Another notification lights up on my screen. *Someone you may know.* My thumb hovers over the picture of an attractive blonde woman and there's a familiarity about her that I can't quite place. With her glossy hair and carefree smile, she could have been me, twenty or so years ago. Back in the days when I didn't appreciate what I looked like or what I was capable of achieving.

Chantelle Wilson. I tap the screen. I know her from somewhere but *where?* She's too old to be one of Hayley's friends, but clearly, if she's come up on my feed, she's someone who's been looking at my profile. Her photos are, of course, perfect in every way. There are certainly no crow's feet or grey streaks on her.

As I get further down her feed, my breath catches. Six photos in, a very familiar sight catches my eye. Even with his back to the camera, I'd recognise Jay anywhere. I watched him closely enough for many months. I knew every angle of him, every essence of his movement. Oh my God – it's really him. This could be the breakthrough I've been waiting for since the second of January when he disappeared into thin air.

I return my attention to the woman and suddenly, I recognise her. She was in my pub on New Year's Eve, standing at the bar and tossing her mane of hair behind her, laughing as she hung onto Jay's every word. I can see now they'll have been laughing at me. I was twisted with jealousy at the time, but then smug because as soon as Jay saw *me*, he turned all his attention away from her. Or so I thought. He made me feel like I was the only woman in the world and I had no idea it was all an act.

So what's going on now?

Chantelle hasn't tagged him *or* any locations in her pictures but judging from the endless exotic backgrounds, sun-drenched lighting, her skimpy swimwear and shapely holiday clothes, she looks to have been in the same place for well over a month. I just need to do some detective work to find out *where* they are. Wherever it is, they're clearly somewhere a million times better than I am, and evidently on *my* dime. Anger fizzes in me like a hangover cure. There has to be some clue – somewhere. I will find them and God help *him* when I do.

I'm almost ready to give up when a video appears in her line of 'stories.'

Can't believe we're buying into the place, says the caption, posted *just now*. I pause the video as she zooms the camera in on herself wearing her perfectly-cut bikini. Bitch. Whatever they're 'buying into...' Hang on. I zoom in on the shopping bag beside her. *Paradis,* it says. Then below it, *Bodrum.*

Bodrum? Of course. That's in Turkey.

My heart's racing now as I return to the first photo that caught my eye. It's *definitely* the woman from New Year and she'll be the one feeling smug now. And it's definitely Jay behind her in the other picture. The paper shopping bag looks pristine and new as though whatever's been bought from 'Paradis' is a recent purchase. And Jay mentioned Turkey when he talked of his upcoming travels – it was somewhere he'd holidayed as a child with his late mother.

With trembling fingers, I open up the app for Booking.com. The trip will have to go on my credit card until Dad's money comes through. Even if I only get half my money back from Jay, it's worth pursuing. And if he won't give me that, well at least I'll have the opportunity to threaten him with the alternative and watch his face fall in person.

We might have been involved in what happened on New Year's Day 'together.' But it was *him* who lit the match that torched the pub – I was back at the care home with Dad and have already proved it to the police. *Jay* ended Bryn's life. I might have been complicit but I've got several cards I can play to explain my involvement if things were to come out. Cards which should mitigate for me. Jay's got no excuse whatsoever. No excuse other than greed.

I'm not bothered about which hotel I stay in. As long as it's reasonably priced and central. I click on the first one listed, not really caring about the photos of its pool or its flower-festooned balconies. It's less than a hundred quid a night which isn't too bad considering we're coming into the summer season. Hopefully, I won't need to stay for too long. With a bit of luck on my side, it won't take long to track Jay down and get what I want from him.

I could message Chantelle – of course I could, but that risks sending them underground and I'll never have the chance to personally deliver my ultimatum then. I wonder if she even realises the connotations of having him in the background of the pictures she's flaunting. She'll have nothing better to do as she lazes around on sunloungers all day. No, the only way is to turn up and take Jay completely by surprise. He'll have been hoping never to set eyes on me again. Part of me can hardly wait to see the look on his face, the other part of me is terrified.

'I've made you some tea and toast, Mum.' I jump as the lounge door swings open and Hayley clatters towards me. 'What are you looking at?' Roles have completely reversed over the last few months. It's been more Hayley looking after me since I've been staying with her and Gemma when it should really be the other way around.

I sweep my thumb to click away from the availability calendar for the hotel but I'm not quick enough.

'Oooh, Bodrum.' She slides the tray onto the table beside me and hangs around behind my armchair. 'I've heard good things about it. We learned when I was at school that it's the only country in the world to sit on two continents. You're not thinking of going, are you?'

'Just looking – you know, perhaps for when Grandad's money comes through.' My face is burning as I stare at the patterns on the carpet. If she notices, I'll just say I'm having yet another hot flush.

'Why wait until then?' She perches on the arm of my chair. She's brushed her hair now and it hangs down her back like a sleek, shiny curtain, just how mine used to look when I was young. 'I've got some money saved up. We could go *together*.'

I stare at her. This isn't what I had in mind at all. I just need to get there, do what I've got to do and then get away again. Quickly and painlessly. At least that's what I'm praying for. I don't know if my already battered conscience will allow me to accept my daughter's savings for this.

'Come on, Mum. We could *both* use a holiday and it would be lovely to spend some proper time together.'

'What about your brother? We can't leave him out. Why don't we book something later in the year when—'

'It's not our fault he's away at uni.' She flicks her hand in the air. 'Besides, now he's back with Sophie, he's supposed to be going away with her this summer, isn't he?'

This is true. It's the only good thing that came out of it all. Lance had been heartbroken after Sophie split with him. But the news of Bryn's death brought her back. And I'm more grateful than I've ever been for the love and support she's shown him. She helped to put the Lance-shaped pieces back together in a way no one else could.

'Why have you only put *four days* into the date checker?' Hayley leans against my arm. 'Change it to at *least* seven days. And change one person into two.'

'Yes, Miss.'

I don't see how I'm going to get out of it. And looking at the situation logically, Hayley offering to use her savings until we get Dad's money through has got to be better than racking up credit card debt and interest fees. At least I'll be able to pay her back once I've done what I've got to do.

Plus she's right. After all she's been through, she really *does* deserve a holiday. I'll just have to get away on my own soon after we arrive. Once I've found out exactly where Jay's 'buying into.' And where he and Chantelle are staying. Hopefully, until we get there, something else on her Facebook profile will give them away to make things easier for me.

I do as Hayley asks. 'Look, there's a twin room available. It's the last one.'

'For the day after tomorrow.' Her voice lifts. 'That's amazing.' She leaps from the arm of the chair, making Sammy jump. 'I'll fetch my bank card.'

Her voice is the lightest and happiest I've heard it for months. I have no choice. I'm going to Bodrum.

With my daughter.

3

DEBRA

'ARE you really sure you don't mind?' I face my friend and former employee, Jennefer in her hallway. I pass her the bag with Sammy's food for a week inside. I always feel bad when I leave Sammy anywhere and can hardly believe I was planning to leave her behind to go travelling with Jay. It wasn't as if it was just a fortnight or a week either. More like a year, or even a lifetime if things had worked out.

'Of course I don't.' She reaches for Sammy's lead and takes the bag from me. 'I'm glad you and Hayley are getting away – you both deserve a break. But I have to ask...' Her smile fades as she hesitates.

'The money I owe you – I know.'

'It's just, well, it's a month's money.' Jennefer tucks her hair behind one ear. 'And you've always said—'

'Hayley's subbing me for the holiday.' I'd hate for her to think I'm spending her wages on going away. 'You know, just until the other money's sorted.'

'From the insurance?' There's hope in her eyes as she waits for my answer.

'Yeah.' I look away. I can hardly tell her it's been refused – not yet anyway. Nor can I tell her that I'm flying to Turkey to force Jay into returning what he stole from me, using what we did to Bryn as leverage. As things stand, nobody suspects my part in the pub fire or my husband's death. Well, nobody except bloody Tina. But, when I get back from Turkey, I'll be able to call her off, once and for all. 'So I should be able to settle up with you and the other staff soon after we get back.'

I owed them *all* a month's wages at the time of the fire. It was all in the bank, ready to transfer but because I'd been away travelling with Lance back to his university, I hadn't got around to sorting it. Then, like an idiot, I trusted Jay with my login details. There was no action I could have taken against him afterwards. He was my bar manager, I'd given him access and I'd authorised him to carry out a transfer.

The one thing I hadn't authorised was him running off with someone else instead of me.

'Have you got time for a cuppa?' Jennefer points to the kitchen. 'I was just about to make myself one.'

'Are you on your own?' I glance behind her. After all, her husband is renowned for not being the friendliest person on the planet and I'm not in the mood for exchanging false pleasantries with *him*.

'Yeah, he's dropping the kids off at breakfast club on his way to work.' Her face darkens as it always does when the subject of Chris comes up. I can only hope that one day she'll see the light and kick him to the kerb.

'I've got ten minutes spare.' I check my watch. 'Our taxi's coming in three-quarters of an hour to collect Hayley and me from her house.'

'I'll get the kettle on then.'

I follow her into the kitchen and Sammy trots behind us. She clearly hasn't realised that I'm leaving her. I glance down at her dear little face and my heart swells like it always does when I look at her. We've been through so much together, this dog and I, and since Bryn's death, she's been my little shadow. I can't help but feel guilty for leaving her but it's only for a week and it isn't like she doesn't know Jennefer well. Jennefer was working at the pub even before we got Sammy. She'll be fine.

Jennefer takes two cups from the cupboard and then swings around to face me. 'I've often wondered if I made things worse with Bryn.' Her voice is uncertain.

'What do you mean?' I frown at her, remembering our chat on New Year's Eve when we had a coffee outside together. How she tried to stop me from *making a big mistake* as she saw it. What I've never been able to tell her since, is just how much of a mistake it all was.

'I've never told you this before...' She looks hesitant as she continues to face me but fixes her gaze on the tiled floor.

'What?' A cold hand of fear clutches at my chest. Surely she doesn't suspect me of anything – other than trusting Tina, I've been really careful to cover my tracks.

'There's no easy way of telling you this but Bryn came onto me – just before he died.'

'What? Really?'

'Yeah – he kind of cornered me in the staff room. I mean, really – it was all I needed, what with everything I was going through with Chris at the time.'

'Oh. Right. When you say, *just* before...'

'I mean, *just* before. Look – I'm sure he didn't mean any harm, he was really drunk but I can't help thinking...'

'What?'

'That if I hadn't been so rotten when he propositioned me, if I hadn't *laughed* at him...' Her voice trails off.

'Please don't tell me you've spent the last four months blaming yourself.' I step towards her.

She hangs her head. 'I must have made things worse for him, Debra. What I said could have been the straw that—'

I grip the sides of her arms and force her to look at me. 'Jennefer, you daft sod. As if you haven't talked to me before about this. *None* of what happened was your fault – do you hear me?'

'But I laughed at him, Deb. At the time, I couldn't believe what he was coming out with. Even if I wasn't friends with you, he couldn't be further from my type.'

'I'm not surprised you laughed – you must have been really uncomfortable.' I let go of her arms so she can get on with making the tea. I wish I could truly put her mind at rest and tell her whose fault it all *really* was. And all because I was the puppet on Jay's string.

I also wish I could talk to her about how Tina's blackmailing me. Before all this, Jennefer and I could tell each other anything. But what I ended up being involved with *has* to stay buried. If it were to come out, it would cost me an awful lot more than what I've lost already. And if I were to lose my kids, I might as well be dead too.

'I bet you're relieved to be getting away from here.' The taxi driver winks as he tugs our case from the car. 'I think you should smuggle me with you.'

'There's barely space in there for all my daughter's shoes as it is.' I smile at Hayley as she wrestles with her umbrella, wishing she'd hurry before we get soaked to the skin. I'm glad my daughter's coming with me – as long as she doesn't find out what I'm up to.

'Bodrum here we come,' she squeals, holding the umbrella over me as I drag the case behind us. In spite of everything, it's wonderful to see her smiling. For weeks I wondered if she'd ever smile again.

I shiver – and it's not just with the murky May weather we're about to leave behind.

4

DEBRA

'YOU OK, MUM?' Hayley offers her arm to steady me as we begin descending the steps from the plane. 'You only had two G&T's, you lightweight.'

'You know I'm not a great traveller,' I say. I've spent the entire flight feeling nauseous. This is normal for me on long journeys, especially on cars and trains but I'm normally not too bad on a plane. This journey, however, has been intensified by what I've got to face within the next day or two. As soon as the plane took off, it all became more real. What if I can't even find him? After all, I'm here on the strength of something I saw on a carrier bag.

'Well we're here now, aren't we?' Hayley tosses her blonde pony-tail behind her shoulder. 'Once we find our hotel, we can just chill. Thanks for agreeing to this, Mum. I think it's going to do us both the world of good.'

'Me too.' I tighten my grip on her arm. My daughter's been my rock through all this. As she often says, she knows what I'm going through. *She lost her dad – then I lost mine.* I just wish this *was* a holiday for us to put ourselves back together and I didn't have to face the inevitable.

But who knows how things could turn out?

Our heels and the wheels of our hand luggage click against the smooth tiles as we make our way towards security. Normally, as soon as the heat envelops me when stepping off a plane, I'm beside myself with excitement and a sense of freedom. But all I feel in my stomach is misery and dread. Perhaps, once I've got my confrontation with Jay over and done with, I can relax into spending a few days of quality time with Hayley. I know she needs them – and really, so do I.

Then Lance's face enters my head. He didn't sound too happy when I spoke to him on the phone last night, even when I promised he and I would do something special together in the holidays. We should have invited him to Bodrum but I didn't want to complicate things more than they already are. Plus, he's missed enough time from university over the last term with everything that's happened to our family and he's also been distracted by his reconciliation with Sophie. And now that I can't support them as well financially as I once could, him doing well at his degree is more important than ever.

I imagine Jay and Chantelle taking this very walk through the airport together, her with her head on his shoulder, saying, *we did it* and him grinning inanely back at her. She *must* have been in it with him all along – and when she was standing in my pub on New Year's Eve, she'll have been laughing at what they had in store for me rather than at something he said, like I thought. She might have been giving pointers throughout all those weeks of him seducing me. There's no other word for it – I was *seduced* by his charisma and his youth. But I wonder if Chantelle knows he went as far as *sleeping* with me in that final week, as she didn't end up staying for very long after I got back on New Year's Eve. I thought Jay wanted me as much as I wanted him.

There's no fool like an old fool. This was one of Dad's favourite sayings.

He wasn't wrong.

'What's Turkish for taxi, Mum?' Hayley slips her cardigan off as we swap the air-conditioned airport for the heat outside. 'Ah this is perfect – some sun at last.'

I point at a sign with a queue of cars snaking from it. 'Let's just hope they take card payments – I never thought to organise any currency.'

'Well, luckily, I did.' Hayley pats her handbag.

'I don't know what I'd do without you.' I smile at her, wishing for the hundredth time that everything was different.

'Oh my God.' Hayley clutches my arm as our taxi weaves in and out of lorries and bikes along the motorway. 'It's like being in Wacky Races. Don't they have to take driving tests here?'

'As if I wasn't feeling sick enough before.' I can't tear my eyes away from the speedometer.

Every muscle in my body clenches as I try to ignore the fact that the driver is texting whilst driving at a hundred and twenty kilometres an hour. I try to shift my focus to the barren mountains surrounding us. I want to sort my phone out – connect it to a Turkish network and check Facebook again. I want to see if Chantelle's posted anything since we boarded our flight – something which might help me pinpoint Jay's exact whereabouts. I'm still none the wiser apart from that shopping bag I saw.

Hayley's as green as I am by the time we're deposited at the side of the road outside our hotel. Then as the driver speeds away, she drags me out of the path of an oncoming moped. The rider shouts something at us as he passes. I fall back against the wall, gasping.

'Come on, Mum.' Hayley shakes her head. 'We're still alive. Let's get in there and celebrate with something strong and alcoholic.'

'I think we need to after that journey.'

'Welcome.' The lady at reception plucks a key from a hook. 'I now show you to your room.'

We follow her along the crazy paving by the side of the pool where guests bask on sun loungers with novels and cocktails. How I'd love to have their normality. I wish I was here just to recuperate with Hayley instead of being here to hunt down the man who reeled me in and ripped me off. The man who lit the match that ended my husband's life. But I was part of it no matter how much I try and distance myself from the reality. I locked the door at the bottom of the stairs to our private quarters. I removed the keys from all the windows. I knew what was happening all along. No matter how desperate to escape our marriage I was, no matter how maddened with grief I was at our children leaving home or how blinded I was with infatuation for the younger man who was showering me with attention, I can never shake off the responsibility that sits squarely on my shoulders. I only hope, that eventually, I find a way to live with the guilt. I only hope that in time, I stop seeing Bryn's face and hearing his voice everytime I try to sleep.

'Well this is even nicer than in the photos.' Hayley casts her eyes over the brightly-coloured twin room and then smiles at the woman. 'Can we order two cocktails on the sun loungers out there?' She points at the window. 'Is that alright with you, Mum?'

'Sure is. I'll just have a quick shower and get into my cozzie.'

By the time I arrive outside, Hayley's just about finished her cocktail.

'Ow, ow, ow.' I hop on my toes towards her. 'I can't believe how hot these flags are. I should have worn my flip-flops.'

'It's a good job you're here, Mum. I was just about to get started on yours as well.' She laughs as she holds her glass towards mine.

'Cheers.' I tap it against hers as I lower myself to the sunlounger.

'Here's to a week of relaxation.'

If only. It's the first holiday we've ever taken – just me and her. The first one we've ever had without Bryn and Lance. Despite the beautiful blue sky and the flowers that surround us everywhere we look, a cloud of melancholy, so dark it's almost choking, creeps over me. I'd do anything to feel better and to feel normal again.

'Right, I'm off for a swim.' Hayley swings her legs around to the side. 'I'll give you chance to catch up with your cocktail before we order another.'

'I'm just going to text Jennefer and check on Sammy,' I tell her.

She grins. 'She'll be fine, Mum. Honestly, you worry too much.'

I watch my daughter for a few moments as her arms propel her up the length of the pool. She's been through so much. She was worn down enough by the end of last year, what with her legal training and then the way Carl had treated her. But then, with what she's had to cope with this year, it's lovely to see her relaxing at last.

I reach for my cocktail, relishing the hit of the alcohol as it warms the back of my throat, then the tang it leaves on my tongue. I can see why Hayley's downed hers so quickly. As soon as I've done what I need to, I'll be ordering us another. The sun's already lowering in the sky so I think the best course of action for the rest of today is to stay here with Hayley, find somewhere close to the hotel for a meal and then try to get a decent night's sleep after our journey. I can only hope I've left the bad dreams behind in York-shire. I need a full night's sleep so badly.

As Hayley continues swimming up and down the pool, I set up the e-sim I bought for my phone and then head over to Facebook. I've just gone the longest I've been without checking it over the last week. Chantelle Wilson's name is at the top of the search results so I immediately click into her profile. Like me, she's got everything set up for everyone and anyone to see. Perhaps, given that Tina found *me* so easily on Facebook too, I should be looking into how to alter my settings so my profile is locked to anyone I'm not 'friends' with.

She's posted a new 'story.' *Another day, another bikini.* It displays a black number that leaves little to the imagination. I glance down at myself. Yes, I've lost weight, but my middle-aged body bears all the stretch marks and cellulite of a woman who's borne two children and not been to a legs, bums and tums class this side of the New Year. How could I have *ever* believed that Jay could prefer me to *her*?

There's a green hue to her skin, suggesting she's under a green parasol and a sign behind her where *ge beach bar* is visible. The *ge* looks as if it's the end of a word.

The red message alert appears in the corner of the screen.

> I'm not going away, Debra. All I'm asking is that we meet to discuss the way forward. Tina.

Bloody woman! I'm certainly getting a taste of what her son did to my daughter with this. Stalking people must run in their family. I hit delete on the message and return to what I was doing. I haven't got the headspace to deal with Tina right now but her messages are certainly becoming more frequent.

Firing up Google, I type *beach bars in Bodrum* and am hit with a list of possibilities. Most have very definite Turkish names. Then, just as I'm about to give up, four from the bottom of the page, I find what I'm looking for. *Dolphini Village Beach Bar.* As I click on images, my breath sharpens when noticing the rows of parasols lining the beach between the building and the shore. They're all green.

It looks like I've found whatever they're 'buying into.' Now all I have to do is approach the place.

Well, *him.*

5

DEBRA

'THIS IS a lovely spot isn't it?' Hayley smiles across the table, her freckled face bathed in the glow of the candlelight as the waiter strides away. She's right. On one side of us we've got Bodrum Castle and at the other, we've got the harbour reflecting the city lights as far as the eye can see.

Chatter and laughter ring out from many of the boats docked nearby and I find myself uncoiling from the tension that has held me prisoner for so long. With the heat softening my muscles and the sea air filling me with fresh oxygen, it's impossible not to relax to some degree. But I'll never be able to let go entirely. Even with what I'm about to face, my conscience with what I'm trying to leave behind will always hold me in its grip.

'I can certainly think of worse places to eat.' I hold my glass in the air. 'Cheers.'

As Hayley raises her own glass, a cloud of sadness enters her eyes. Just when I think she's going to point out the absence of Lance and Bryn, I realise she's watching a labrador-cross which is wandering from table to table, clearly hunting for scraps.

'They're everywhere.' She points at another one. 'Look, there's four, five, six of them here. Gemma told me about the problem with stray dogs and cats but I didn't realise it was so bad.'

I glance up at the hill to the castle where there must be at least eight skinny cats roaming around as well. My thoughts drift to Sammy. 'It's heartbreaking,' I agree, trying to force my attention away from these animals and back onto my daughter. If I allow myself to become consumed with my sympathy for the strays, I'll become overwhelmed. I'm only just holding my head above water as it is.

'Here, Mum, let's have a selfie to send to Lance. I can't believe we haven't taken one since we got here.'

'Ah no, that, might be rubbing salt into the wounds. You heard how Lance's voice dropped when he found out we were coming here.'

'Well, let's have a selfie together anyway. We don't have to send it to anyone, do we?' Hayley leans into me and holds her phone in front of us. 'Smile, for goodness sake, Mum, we're supposed to be enjoying ourselves.'

Are we? I want to say. But then she doesn't know what I'm really here for or what I'm waiting on. An outcome which has the potential to make or break things for me. I haven't been this desperate for money since I was trying to scrape the funds together for the pub back in my twenties. But back then, I had youth on my side and starting again from scratch didn't feel nearly as daunting as it does now. This could be my last chance for any sort of comeback before I'm put out to pasture.

'It's ace here,' Hayley cries as we walk back to the hotel. It would seem she's let her misery at the stray animals go for now. They've certainly done well from the Adana Kebab Hayley ordered and the Kofte which looked delicious on the menu but I could hardly stomach once it arrived in front of me.

'It's as though the place is only just coming alive.

'You buy?' One of the many shopkeepers lined up along the mall tries to lure us into his handbag shop.

'Not today, thanks,' I tell him.

'You English?' The shopkeeper outside the shoe shop next to him strikes his heart, exuding such warmth towards us that I almost feel like succumbing to his welcome and buying new sandals from him. But I'm too exhausted to pick anything out reliably.

'We'll have to come back tomorrow, Mum.' Hayley's eyes shine as man after man continues to jostle for our custom as we head toward our hotel. We both look as pale as the page and it's probably obvious that we've just stepped off a plane from England. 'Oh.' She pauses. 'Just listen to that.'

It's impossible not to. The ethereal call to the mosque rings out from both ends of the city through the loudspeakers. It's an almost ghostly sound that only adds to my melancholy state. Jay, wherever he is, will be able to hear it too. I picture him with Chantelle and my insides sag some more.

As we weave in and out of shopkeepers, tourists and men trying to drag us into their restaurants, I wonder what I'd do if I suddenly saw Jay. It's not as if I can wear my sunhat and sunglasses in the evening, so he'd notice me immediately if our paths crossed. Which is the last thing I want to happen, particularly with Hayley at my side. It has to be just me and him, somewhere quiet, where I can make him see how there's only one way to resolve all this.

I'm frozen solid. Hayley must have turned the air conditioning up to full after I dropped off. I point the remote control at the unit above our beds, enjoying the warmth returning to my arms and shoulders as I tug the skinny blanket over me.

The sun's already streaming around the edges of our curtains and the crickets have come back to life. I glance at my watch. It's nearly quarter past six. Which means, if we were still in England, it would be quarter past four. I slam my head back against the pillow, praying the reprieve of sleep will find me again. It doesn't, but a hot flush does instead. Damn menopause. Damn being middle-aged. I hate it and would give anything to have the youth of bloody Chantelle Wilson.

I kick the blanket back off me and set the air conditioning going again. I glance over at my daughter, sleeping so peacefully in the other bed. I can't recall the last time I slept like that but at least I seem to have left my bad dreams at home.

Sighing, I reach for my phone and haul myself up to sitting. It's become an almost reflex action to go straight onto Facebook and onto the profile of Chantelle Wilson whenever I pick up my phone. My heart quickens as I notice she's posted another story. They're on a boat, she's surrounded by a sea of smiling faces and at the back, yes it's him again. All tan and white teeth. I bet he wouldn't have posed for the picture if he'd known it might end up on social media. He might have no idea – after all, he's deleted the profile he used to have. But perhaps, away from England and out here in Bodrum, he believes he's invincible. Maybe, he thinks I'll have given up on him by now.

As if.

An image of the harbour where we ate last night fills my mind. As we enjoyed our meal, Jay and Chantelle were perhaps closer than I thought. So today's the day when I'll find him. I've got to get it over with.

I pound up and down the pool in a similar way to how Hayley did last night. For a few sweet minutes, as I breathe in the scent of the pretty pink flowers which surround me, I can almost pretend that I'm just here on holiday, setting myself up for a lovely day with an early morning swim. The temperature's already up and no doubt Hayley will want to spend the day exploring, so I need to think of a reason to break away for a couple of hours.

'There you are.' She steps from our balcony in a long, flowing dress, sunhat and flip-flops. She's quite the catch, my daughter, and I'm just so relieved she saw the light with that bloody Carl, and is now free to meet somebody decent and worthy of her. For a time, she allowed him to really get to her and was becoming more and more cut off from her friends, her interests and even us, her family. I don't know what finally persuaded her to believe what everyone else had seen all along but it still took months to shake him off, even after she'd ended things. Thankfully she has no idea that he's hanging around again – this time around *me*, and with his mother in tow.

'Breakfast's included in the cost of the hotel, isn't it?' She points over at the outdoor seating. 'All this sea air's making me hungry.'

My own stomach rumbles as I pull myself up the steps from the pool, having only picked at my meal last night. But again the reason I'm here hits me, and a stab of nausea replaces my hunger pang. Ever since the New Year, I can't eat. Guilt's hollowed me out.

'Are you just going to play with that?' Hayley points to where I'm pushing chunks of fruit around my bowl. I should be devouring my breakfast. I've never tasted fruit as good as it tastes here, especially the figs. But my appetite has totally vanished. 'What's wrong, Mum?' Once again, it's as though she's the parent and I'm the child.

'Apart from the usual – nothing,' I reply. Really, I'm trying to come up with a reason why I need to get away on my own this morning. The plan is to return to the row of beach bars we walked by last night and look for Dolphini Village with its green umbrellas. 'To be honest,' I go on. I'm just going to come out and say it. 'I'm still feeling a bit peaky. If you don't mind, I'm going to take a walk out after breakfast, get myself back together and then we'll spend the rest of the day together.'

'What? You want to walk on your own?' She frowns. 'But why? If you just give me ten minutes to get sorted, we can take a walk out together.'

'I could do with a bit of me-time,' I insist, trying to load an apology into my voice. 'Just to get my head straight. I didn't sleep too well last night.'

'Without me?' She pulls a face. 'But I'd like to explore too.'

'I'll only be a couple of hours.'

'What if I stay really quiet and don't talk?'

I laugh. 'Impossible. Look, love – I promise I won't be too long. You can chill out here for a bit, can't you? When was the last time you got a chance to read without interruption?'

'True,' she replies, wrinkling her nose. 'I wouldn't mind getting stuck into that Frenemy novel I picked up at the airport.'

'There you go then. And I'll be back before you know it.'

She narrows her eyes as she continues to study me. 'I know that look, Mum. What are you really up to?'

'Nothing, love. Honestly.'

6

DEBRA

DOLPHINI VILLAGE BEACH BAR is the first bar in the row. Before I do anything, it makes sense to ensure that I have the right place. Tugging my sun hat over my eyes, I loiter not far from the entrance towards the sun loungers, pretending to be engrossed in a boat trip timetable whilst stealing glances towards the bar as joggers periodically dart across my line of vision.

It's fairly empty in there but then I suppose it's still early. Bodrum, as the hotelier told us at breakfast, mostly comes alive at night. The locals are late risers, as after all, it's often so hot during the day that they have completely different body clocks to us English.

There's no sign of Jay or Chantelle. I close my eyes for a moment. Just putting their names together in my mind provokes a tug of depression in the pit of my belly. It should have been Jay and Debra. We'd planned to start our travels in India and when I think back to the way he used to look at me and the conversations we had, I still find it difficult to believe it was all an elaborate lie to separate me from my money.

If they've been here right from the time when he first took off in January, their body clocks are no doubt also set to Turkish time so they could be still sleeping. Therefore, I might be hanging around here for a long time yet. I'll have to get in there and at least establish that I'm on the right lines. I'll be able to get someone to tell me something, surely?

I'm shaking from the inside out as I head onto the pebbled beach, unsure of how or even whether I want to attract attention to myself. This feels extremely risky. It *is* extremely risky.

'You lunch here?' A man, clearly local, appears from behind one of the rows of loungers waving a menu.

'Erm no. I've not long since eaten breakfast.' I rub at my belly as I laugh. 'Can I just have some coffee for now?'

'Ah, yes, no problem. Have seat? Would you like shade or sun?'

I point at a single lounger beneath one of the green shades. Looking along the entire row, I see this is the only beach bar with green shades. I *must* have the right place. Perhaps I should have ordered chamomile tea or even wine instead of coffee. I'm jangling enough as it is. I settle down to wait for it, slipping my flip-flops off and arranging my dress around me. Apart from being a million shades paler than anyone else around here, I look like just another traveller on a sunlounger to anyone who doesn't know me.

By the time he returns with my coffee, I'm reasonably satisfied that he's the only waiter serving here this morning. So I need to ask him about Jay.

'I'm a friend of Chantelle's,' I announce as he sets the coffee cup on the table next to me.

He looks puzzled and then a look of recognition enters his eyes. 'Ah, yes, beautiful Chantelle. And yes, you're from England too. She not say friend coming.'

'I want to surprise her,' I tell him. 'And Jay. They don't know I'm here yet.'

'You mean Jayden,' he replies, gesturing towards the boats moored up along the sea wall. *That's* where he must be staying. Who knew all this could be so easy? We've only been in the country since yesterday and already I'm closing in on him.

Jayden. When I once asked him what Jay was short for, his reply was that it wasn't short for *anything*. Really, I didn't know him at all – only what he *wanted* me to know.

'They work here?' I lift my voice at the end so he knows it's a question but try to keep my voice nonchalant so he has *no* idea of how much I've got riding on it.

'You drink?' He points at my cup but I don't want to drink my coffee yet. The shake of my hand could give away how anxious I am. 'No, Jayden, he will own with me after the sale.'

'Oh, right.' I nod. 'And will they be here today?'

'Yes.' He checks his watch. 'We have meeting. Chantelle, ah she likes the sun and the swim.' He points at the cordoned area of ocean stretching in front of the row of beach bars. 'Jayden, we talk the business. You know them from England?' His English is stilted but very good, making me feel bad for not learning at least a few basic Turkish words while we're staying here.

'Yes.' I'm not going to elaborate any further. I don't know what to do for the best. Jay's going to be shocked enough to see me and really, to secure the best possible outcome for myself, I need to speak to him somewhere quiet where we won't be interrupted. Somewhere on our own but not too remote where I'll be more vulnerable. Do I wait here or is that too brazen? I can't decide.

'Is Jayden staying close by?' I point at the boats. Yes, I'm playing guessing games but I'm certain he'll be on one of those after this man nodded towards them before.

'He sleeps on my boat.' The man points to the other side of the cordoned off area. '*Bodrum Belle.* She needs someone there all night – it is the law here that someone sleeps on board the boats in the port – but my wife, see, she prefers our house.'

So Jay really has fallen on his feet. A place to stay and a business partnership. All in less than four months. Well he might think he's fallen on his feet. He'll be changing his mind when he sees me.

'What time will he be here?' I point at my watch.

'I erm, um – one hour from now – at eleven.' He shrugs. 'What is your name?'

'Erm, Jenny.' Jennefer's name flashes into my head as I give the first name that comes to mind. 'Don't tell them I called here, as like I said, I want to surprise them.'

He strikes his chest with the heel of his hand in a similar way to what I've seen lots of Turkish men do. 'I'll come back then. Can I pay now?' I point at my coffee.

One hour later, I'm reclined on a lounger in the next beach bar up from Dolphini Village, with a glass of wine to settle my shredded nerves. I'm well hidden beneath my large sunglasses and floppy sunhat, so he won't notice me until I'm ready to reveal myself.

Jay was always punctual so it comes as no surprise when at 10:59, he saunters down the side of the building, arm in arm with Chantelle. She's shorter than she appears on social media, petite against Jay's larger frame, bronzed and beautiful.

As she stretches out on one of the loungers, I pretend to busy myself on my phone, but continue watching over there. My breath catches as Jay strides over to her and places a glass of something pink at her side before dropping a kiss on the top of her head. I forgot how good the man looks in a white t-shirt.

What are you thinking, you stupid woman? I give myself a shake as I remember what he's done to me. How he just disappeared into thin air, not only leaving me penniless but also leaving me in the aftermath of what he'd caused by striking that match. With a police investigation, a devastated son and daughter and nowhere to go.

Leaving Chantelle on the lounger to no doubt preen and pose for more pointless stories and posts on Facebook, Jay bounds back towards the building, just in time for his eleven o'clock meeting. Meanwhile, I've been gone for two hours.

Only me, Hayley. I got caught up wandering around the shops. Anyway, I'm just about to order some coffee so I should be back in an hour. xx

I glance at the time. That's possibly a little optimistic but she's going to start getting tetchy with me if I don't get this resolved soon and get back there. She might be in her twenties, but she's been a hell of a lot more anxious and keen to be close to me since the New Year. I abandoned Hayley and Lance on the night when our pub burnt down and they didn't know whose body had been dragged out of there. They both needed me more than they've ever needed me that night so I still have a lot of making up to do.

So, as soon as Jay's on his own, I need to get to him, say what I've got to say, and get away from here. And if getting the police involved isn't a threat enough for him, I can also threaten him with letting his business partner and customers know how dodgy he is and what he's capable of. The guy I spoke to clearly thinks he's dealing with someone he can count on.

Which is exactly what I thought.

7

DEBRA

I'M ALMOST dizzy from averting my eyes between my phone and the door Jay's gone through. As I've been waiting, Chantelle hasn't posted anything else on her page. How I'd love to post a picture of my view and tag her in it with the caption, *gotcha.*

Finally, after twenty minutes, the man who gave me a coffee, and then let me have it at *no charge* because I'm a friend of Chantelle's, comes out. I just hope I haven't been mentioned. At least, not yet.

I drain my wine before sliding my feet back into my sandals. It's now or never. This could be one of the only chances I have when I'm not with Hayley to speak to him. Sliding my phone into the side pocket of my dress, I then sling my bag crossways over my chest and head back towards where I started. The wine's partially settled my nerves but I'm still shaking as I approach the gate which leads back onto the pebbles. As it happens, my timing is perfect.

'Hello, stranger.' I catch his arm as he emerges through the door. I forgot how firm and muscular his arms were.

He swings around and lifts his sunglasses up over his head as though needing to see me clearly. The confusion in his eyes turns to shock. 'Oh, it's *you.*'

'It certainly is. I've been dreaming of this moment for the last four months.'

'Go in there.' He jerks his thumb at the door from which he's just come out of, checking around us as he speaks.

'Anyone would think you didn't want us to be seen together, Jay.' I step in the direction he's pointing. 'But Bryn's dead as you very well know. So we don't have to sneak around anymore.'

'In there. *Now*.' His voice is a hiss and I've never seen him look so rattled. 'Go on.' He gestures towards another room. 'I can't bloody believe this.'

'Perhaps I'd rather stay where I can see the door,' I reply, not taking my eyes off him. 'After all, you've well and truly proven that you can't be trusted.'

'What is it you want, Deb?' He closes the door, muffling the voices in the kitchen as he leans against the bar. 'And how have you found me?'

'Don't call me that.' It's my turn to hiss. 'You've betrayed me in the worst way possible. You don't get to call me *Deb* anymore.'

'Look, I'm sorry, but really, if you're honest with yourself, you always knew who I *really* am.' He shrugs as he glances out of the window towards where Chantelle is lying face down, her head in the opposite direction. All she has to do is spin around and she'll see us in here.

'What, a liar, a murderer and a cheat?' I've imagined this moment for all these months, and now we're actually facing each other, I can hardly believe I've found him.

'A free spirit.' He shrugs again. 'I needed money. I only did what I had to do.'

'*You* killed my husband.' Beads of sweat are rolling from my armpits and down the sides of my body towards the waistband of my dress. The heat is even more oppressive in here than it is outside. I don't know how anyone stands to live in Turkey permanently.

His laughter echoes around the room. 'Ah come on, Deb. You

can't pretend you're not happy to be free of him.' He takes his sunglasses from his head and runs his fingers through his spiky hair. In spite of all he's done to me, I find myself longing to do the same. 'And besides, it was only a case of me getting there first. If I hadn't burned him to a crisp, he was planning to do the same to me, as everyone already knows. So if you're hoping I feel any guilt about it, I can assure you I don't.'

'You've got *no* idea what you've put me through. My dad died last month as well.' I can't believe I'm even telling Jay this. What's got into me? I need to say what I came here to say – never mind spinning him the sob story. If he had an ounce of compassion, he wouldn't have done what he did in the first place.

'I'm sorry to hear that but I don't know—'

'You took everything I had, Jay.' I look him straight in the eyes. 'Nearly eighty grand – the cash, the safe, my account.' I could add my dignity to this list but I don't.

'You knew I needed money. But I never really planned to take it *all*. You have to believe that.' This could be promising. Perhaps he *will* agree to give me some of it back.

'So that makes everything alright, does it?'

'You literally handed it to me on a plate. You know what I'm like, Deb.' He hooks his thumbs into the waistband of his shorts and it's an effort to keep looking into his face. 'I'm never one to pass up an opportunity.'

'I want it back. As you'll have worked out, that's the reason I'm here.' I'm starting by demanding the full amount to allow room for negotiation.

'No can do. It's all tied up in this place now.' He sweeps his arms around, his voice edged with what could possibly be pride.

'Not yet, it isn't.' I step closer to him. 'You're *buying in*. You haven't *bought in* yet.'

His relaxed expression changes to something I can't read. 'Who told you that?'

'I've done my research. Look, Jay, I'm not being unreasonable here. You give me fifty grand of my money back and I'll get out of your hair and return to England.' As I say it out loud, I think I'm being *very* reasonable. I'm giving him thirty grand when really, he should be locked up in a prison cell, serving a life sentence.

'I can't do it.'

'You'll never hear from me again. I think that's very fair under the circumstances.'

'I can't do it,' he repeats, his face and his voice more insistent this time.

'You have to. Or else—'

'Or else, *what?*' His tone completely changes. 'Go on, tell me how you're planning to *make me.*'

'You either pay me my money or I'm going to the police.' My voice shakes as I say it. Even though I'll be implicating myself, it's the only leverage I have. I'll say Jay coerced me – I'll tell them how scared I was. Not just of Bryn but of him as well. Though really, it's the last thing I want to do.

'You may not have noticed but we're in Turkey now, Debra. Different rules apply here.' His voice relaxes as his eyes dart towards the window. 'The police here are hardly going to be interested in anything I got up to in England.'

'*What you got up to?* You mean arson, murder, deception and theft.'

'It's hardly deception and theft when you willingly gave me your login details, Deb. As well as access to the safe.'

'Not so you could rob it all and leave me behind, I didn't. I really thought we had something, when all the time you were stringing me along. I still can't believe—'

'Look, you're obviously a great woman and all that, but really, you were always too old for me.'

'Unlike *Chantelle*, you mean?'

His face darkens as his eyes dart back towards the window. 'How do you know about her?'

'Like I said, I've done my research. Look, I just want my money

– and I'm not going back home without it.' My eyes follow his as I lick the salty sweat off my upper lip. I'm more than ready to march outside and have it out with her out there as well. She's been enjoying the spoils of my money as much as he has.

'I've already told you – it's all gone.'

'Perhaps your new business partner' – I wave my arms to where he's writing someone's order down which might mean he'll be back in here at any minute. – '*And* all your customers outside would like to know exactly what sort of lowlife they're dealing with.' I step towards the door and he grabs my arm, digging his fingers into the flesh of my bicep. The last time he touched me – well I don't even want to think about that.

'You're going too far, Deb.'

'Take your bloody hand off me now or I'm going to yell out for help.' I shake myself out of his grip.

'What's bloody got into you?' There can be no denying I've rattled him. And for some reason my threat of going outside and broadcasting it all seems to have been far more effective than my threat of involving the police.

'I just want my money. I'm not going away, Jay, and make no bones about it – I'm ready to tell anyone and everyone who'll listen what sort of person you really are.'

'You wouldn't—'

'I've got nothing left to lose, thanks to you. I'm staying in my daughter's spare room, the insurance won't pay out because of the circumstances of Bryn's death, and—'

'OK, OK.' His voice softens slightly as he waves his arms around. 'Look, just give me some time, say a day or two, to get my head around things. I can't just magic fifty grand out of thin air, can I?'

'No, but if I let you off the hook now, you could disappear into the thin air you've just mentioned.'

'I'm not going anywhere. Like I said, I'm committed to this place. Tell me where I can reach you?'

'Like I'm really going to tell *you* where I'm staying?' I delve into my bag for one of my old business cards. *Debra Ford, Proprietor, The Dales Inn.* From the days when I was a someone rather than the nobody I've become over the last few months. 'My number's on there.'

'I'll call you then.' He slides the card into his pocket. 'Now go, please – quickly. Chantelle's on her way in.'

I glance towards where she's stretching her limbs out as she rises from her sun lounger, her eyes fixed on the window. Jay seems keen to keep us apart so perhaps she doesn't know the *whole* truth of what he's been capable of.

I pat my pocket as I stride towards the door, reassuring myself that my phone's still there. Then I lower my sunglasses and the rim of my hat. I don't wish to get into anything with *her*. Not yet, anyway. For now, I've got what I came for. Half a promise of an agreement from him but just as important, I've got a recorded conversation that does *everything* to incriminate Jay but where *nothing's* been said which directly incriminates me.

Nothing at all. Our discussion couldn't have gone any better. I've *really* got something to threaten him with now.

8

DEBRA

'YOU'VE BEEN GONE all morning, Mum.' Hayley's sulky pout reminds me of when she was a toddler and I used to collect her from nursery. It would take her until we got home to forgive me for leaving her. 'I've nearly read an entire book while you've been gone.' She flings it to the front of her sun lounger.

'So what are you moaning at then?' I keep my voice light and airy. 'You said you wanted to get through it.' There can be no denying that I feel slightly better since my encounter with Jay, especially at the clear-as-a-bell recording I've managed to obtain of his admission to the absolute lot. I'm just trying not to feel too old and foolish after his blatant rejection of me when we talked. Try as I might, I'm struggling to overcome the infatuation I had for him.

Even if I don't get fifty grand, as near to it as possible would help me to no end right now. I'm only giving him twenty-four hours, and even if he disappears from the beach bar, at least I know where he's staying. While I wait, I need to get this voice recording backed up to the cloud and emailed to myself. It's the only concrete proof I have of anything.

I can't help but think that he must have far more money than what he swindled from me. He told me when I took him on at the

47

pub that he'd already been saving for a while. Plus, he could have sold his possessions, including his motorbike before he scarpered from England.

'I'd have thought you were having a look around the shops?' Hayley points to my empty hands as she sits up.

'I decided I'd rather look around them with you. You'll have more nerve for bartering than I have.' I laugh.

But she doesn't. Her face doesn't change as she reaches for her drink. If I know my daughter correctly, she could remain cross with me for the rest of the afternoon.

'Come on, Hayley. I wouldn't fly into a sulk if you fancied a couple of hours to yourself.'

'Three and a half hours, to be precise.' She taps the face of her watch. 'Look...' The sharp edge leaves her voice. 'I'm just worried about you.' She nods towards the sun lounger next to hers as though wanting me to sit so I lower myself to the edge of it.

'Why?'

'I thought getting away would do you some good but you seem more on edge than ever.'

'I'm sorry. I'm just missing your grandad, I guess.'

She gives me a funny look. 'You've said yourself that you lost him a long time ago. I know it's more final now, but you said you were OK. If you're struggling, how are we meant to know if you don't tell us?'

'Let's just change the subject, shall we?'

'And you never mention Dad. Not ever. It's like he's become a taboo subject. Lance thinks so too.' She tosses her hair behind one shoulder. 'Every time we try to talk about him, you close us down. Don't think we don't notice.'

'It's not like that at all – it's just, well, it's still all so raw, isn't it?' This is the understatement of the century. 'Look, how about we get you out of here, you've clearly had too much time to brood this morning. Let's find somewhere really posh for lunch and have a nice, girly afternoon?' The truth is that I can't bear to discuss Bryn with her. I'm always worried she'll see something in my eyes which will give me away.

'OK, I guess breakfast was quite a while ago.' She pats her hand against the flat of her belly. I remember when my belly looked like that – many, many moons ago. And it seems that no amount of sit-ups or dieting will gift me a midriff like that again.

'Right, I'm just going to get changed and slap some sun cream on.'

I'm glad we're doing something. I need to keep busy while Jay gets my money together. I feel certain that my silence will be worth enough to him to put his hand deeply into his pocket in order to get rid of me. And if I sense any problems or him trying to stall, I'll just send him a copy of my recording.

'I fancy one of those beach bars we walked past yesterday,' Hayley says as we head out of the gate. 'The lady here told me that we just need to buy something from them and then we can have the loungers for the rest of the day.'

I already know this from this morning's visit. 'I was thinking more of a cafe or a restaurant. I mean, wouldn't you rather sit at a table to eat?' Going anywhere near the beach bars feels risky, even if I steer Hayley in the opposite direction from where Jay is. If she claps eyes on him for one second, I'll be rumbled.

'No, I really fancy it, actually.' Hayley pouts like she always does when she's fighting for her own way. Really, I should be glad that she's suddenly found her backbone after a lifetime of people-pleasing tendencies. 'We'll be in the shade and we've got the sea to keep ourselves cool.'

I have to admit that I'm tempted too, now she puts it like that. And I guess there are at least a dozen of the bars along that stretch so as long as we stay where we are for the afternoon with no wandering around, the chances of running into Jay are minimal.

Being in such close proximity might help with keeping an eye on his activities and whereabouts.

~

'Ah, this is the life.' Hayley stretches her feet out on her lounger and takes a photo of her pretty pink-painted toenails with the sea beyond them. As Hayley continues to fiddle around on her phone, I slide mine from my bag. Just in case he's been in touch already. He *hasn't* but my heart sinks at who *has*.

> I can't believe you're continuing to ignore me, Debra. I was a friend to you on that train journey and I've kept your sordid little secrets for all this time. If you don't get back in touch by the end of today with a way forward from this, I'll be forced to go to the police with everything I know. Tina.

'I'll just have a swim while we wait for lunch to arrive.' I tug my dress over my head, grateful I've already got my costume on and don't have to find somewhere to change. 'I'm absolutely roasting.' Really, I need to process this message and work out how I'm going to handle it. I can't keep burying my head. Sooner or later, I'll have to face the woman. It just so happens that the one thing she needs and wants from me is the thing I'm completely unable to give her.

'I'd better wait here with the phones and bags then, hadn't I?' Hayley sounds gloomy again. It's as though she can't bear to let me out of her sight today. A stab of guilt pierces me. After all, it's *my* fault she's already lost one of her parents and is clinging to me – the one who's left. Plus, in the aftermath of it all, because I so selfishly disappeared with Jay on New Year's Day, she spent a good fifteen or sixteen hours fearing it was *me* who might be dead.

'They said lunch would be around half an hour, so I'll just go off for quarter of an hour or so, then you can have a turn before we eat.' That should be long enough to swim into the vicinity of the green umbrellas. And there are enough swimmers in the stretch of sea that's been cordoned off to protect me from being seen by Jay.

'OK – go and cool off then.'

I get in up to my knees, then my waist, looking back at Hayley with a grimace. 'It's chillier than it looks,' I call. However, if I want to get back here so Hayley can swim before our lunch arrives, I need to get going.

The mouthful of salt water comes as a shock as I gasp at the sudden rush of cold. But then, as I become accustomed to the water, my body relaxes into the waves as I dart through them. I reach the end of the line of our orange umbrellas and continue into the red ones, weaving in and out of the lilos and people chasing each other through the clear blue water with shrieks of laughter.

The call for mosque echoes around, a sound I'm becoming accustomed to. It's echoed around several times already since sunrise. Lulled by the lap of the waves, I keep going, sending myself out at a diagonal from the shoreline. I can only hope Hayley doesn't swim this way when she takes her turn. Though I doubt she will swim as far down as I'm planning to.

As I leave the area of red umbrellas and enter the yellow ones, I wonder why I don't do this more often. At the ripe old age of fifty, this is the first time I've ever swum in the ocean. Most of our holidays over the years have been at all-inclusive resorts with a pool. That's when we even permitted ourselves to take holidays. When you're the owner of a pub, time off is difficult.

The waves are picking up by the time I reach the green umbrellas and I pause, turning towards the shore as I tread water and try to keep my head above the surface. This has been the story of my life for the last few months.

There's no sign of Jay unless he's inside, but Chantelle is in the same place she was earlier. Is this what she does *all* day? Sits around in the sun, revolving her life around whatever Jay's doing and posting on social media? It might be alright for a day or three but would soon become boring. If I'd come away with him, like we were supposed to, I'd have done something with my life. I wouldn't have just lazed around, posing in a bikini for selfies all day, even if I looked like she does.

Her being here without him might be a positive sign. If he was taking orders and waiting on loungers, it would mean that he's not actively working on pulling my fifty grand together. By this time tomorrow, I'll be able to make an offer to Tina and get rid of her forever. I suppose I'll have to message her back. See if I can buy myself more time.

9

TINA

'I can't believe we're actually here.' Carl stares from the window of the bus as I mop sweat from my brow. 'Hayley's face is going to be a picture when she sees *me*.'

'We're not here for you to see Hayley, are we?'

'Nope, but once the money stuff's sorted...' The rest of his sentence is drowned out by the roar of the bus's engine as it's started up.

'I still haven't a clue how to handle it.' Hysteria rises as my lack of planning hits me. Travelling here has been on a whim and I'd hit the *book now* button before I'd given myself the chance to really consider the implications.

'Have you let Dad know we've taken off like this?'

'No.' I resist the urge to remark on how he doesn't let me know when he's going off with his fancy woman. It's not as if his father's exploits would be news to Carl though. For me, the fact that Pete's so blatant about it makes it all the more hurtful. It's little wonder Carl and Amanda are often so disrespectful towards me – after all, they've had a master of a teacher in their father. Having said that, when I announced to Carl what we were doing, I saw a respect in his eyes that I hadn't seen for a long time. Perhaps he felt proud that for once in my life, I was actually standing up and being counted. And to say how condescending and distant he normally can be towards me, things between us have been pretty amicable since we left Yorkshire.

I twiddle my rings around as the bus pulls away from the airport. The rings I've worn for so long now feel as though they're burning into my finger. I don't even know why I wear them anymore – our marriage certificate has never been worth the paper it's written on.

'How long did you book Grandma into respite for in the end?'

'Three nights. That should be long enough for us to do what we've got to do here. And time enough to get the money we've taken back into her account before anyone realises it's missing.' Something within me plummets at the memory of what I've done. But I'm desperate. Pete's made it perfectly clear he wants a divorce, and is intending to sell the house from under me. Meanwhile, I can't even afford a solicitor to get some advice.

'So what's the plan?'

I was hoping Carl might come up with some ideas instead of leaving it all to me. But, clearly not.

'I haven't got that far yet but the first thing is to find out where they're staying. I could do with Hayley tagging them in somewhere again.'

'Has Debra replied to that last message yet?'

'Hang on. I haven't checked since we landed.' I reach into my bag. 'Oh bloody hell. We're not covered here – we're not in the EU, are we? It's going to cost a bomb to get online.' I'm sick of living like this. Always worrying about money and never able to afford anything.

'Well, you'll just have to borrow some more from Grandma's account.'

I glance around at our neighbouring passengers. They're mostly jabbering away in Turkish. I don't want to even *think* about syphoning more money from my mother's account. 'No, finding

Debra is our best bet. We already know *roughly* where she is from that post Hayley tagged her in.'

'How close is it to where we're getting dropped off?' Carl glances at his watch.

'Without being able to get on and look at Google Maps, I'm not sure exactly – but pretty close.' I turn my phone over in my hand. I feel lost without being able to get onto the internet.

'At least she won't be able to ignore us anymore.' Carl shakes his head.

'She was pleading poverty when I collared her at her husband's funeral and yet she's jetting off somewhere like this for a holiday. That insurance money *must* have come through.' The main reason we need to find her before she goes and spends it all.

'Either that or she's chasing after that Jay one. Didn't she tell you that he'd taken all her money when you were speaking to her and probably gone abroad?'

> Since you're able to afford a holiday in Bodrum, you must have all your money. And since you haven't contacted me or answered my mum's messages, I'm on my way to see you. Sort my money or I'm telling Hayley EVERYTHING.

'It's been delivered.' Carl thrusts his screen in front of me. His Messenger app is showing as *offline*. I stare at the *delivered* notification which appeared just before he had to put his phone into airplane mode.

'She'll have had the shock of her life when she read that.'

'She'll ignore it anyway.' His face darkens. 'She won't believe I'd turn up here.'

'Well, firstly we need to find somewhere to stay on a night-by-night basis and then we'll track *her* down.' I stare out of the window. We've passed some lovely-looking hotels, obviously well out of our price range. Who knows what we'll be able to afford with the meagre amount I've dared to take from my mother's account?

'We're going to collar Debra on her own to start with, aren't we?'

'Definitely. We should give her one last chance to pay up before we tell Hayley everything we know. And we should stick to what we said, you deal with Debra and if and when the time comes, I'll deal with Hayley.'

'I never knew you had this in you, Mum.'

'Says the man who was being paid to torch a pub with someone inside.' I nudge his arm.

The truth is that I didn't know I had it in me either. But we can't go on having nothing and being treated like nobodies. I finally snapped when I discovered how they'd used Carl like they had and then not paid him a penny.

'Yeah, but I didn't in the end, did I? How much are we trying to squeeze out of her anyway? Have we decided?'

'Well, there's the five grand which you should have got from him on New Year's Day. But now there's the matter of expenses with having to follow them over here, plus if she's either found her toy-boy or had her insurance payout— I suggest we go in high, to be honest.'

'Do you honestly think she'll cough up?' Carl looks sceptical. 'I still don't. I just hope we're not wasting our time.'

'I guess it depends on how much she doesn't want her daughter to know the truth.' This is all we've got. I guess we *could* also threaten her with the police but then there's the problem of implicating Carl.

'I still think our biggest problem is that it's all your word against hers. You've got no proof of that conversation you had with her on the train.'

If only I could get hold of the man who'd been sitting in front of us as we travelled from Leicester to Yorkshire that day. He turned around several times. The couple of gins Debra drank evidently loosened her tongue and gave him cause for an extremely raised eyebrow at me as we got off the train at Leeds. Maybe, if it ever became necessary, he could somehow be tracked down.

'We'll cross that bridge when we come to it.' I drop my phone back into my bag. 'Anyway, I've had enough of people like her,' I continue. I glance at my son who looks to be deep in thought. 'I know it's reckless, us catching that flight like we did. But the minute I saw Debra's face smiling out of that photo, I knew we had to do *something*. She helped to murder her husband and now she's swanning around in places like this.' I gesture from the window at the ocean and it gleams back at us. 'And all the time, she's sticking two fingers up at us. I've given her plenty of time to sort something out.'

It's a good job the other passengers on this bus can't understand me. Especially with my use of words like murder.

'How many times have *you* messaged her now?' Carl gestures at my bag. 'I must have sent around six over the last couple of weeks.'

'Oh, it must be around a dozen. But I did leave her alone for a while after the funeral. This week, I've messaged her every day so far and she's completely ignored me. She needs to remember that one word to the police could send her to prison.'

'But it could send me there too, Mum.' He jerks his thumb towards himself. 'Don't forget that.'

'I know, which is why I haven't done it yet.' I lean into him as the bus turns a sharp corner. 'But the bottom line is that you didn't actually *do* anything. Not like she did. Every single thing she told me on that journey – it all came to pass.'

'But we keep coming back to the same thing – what proof have you got of what she told you?'

'I know – which is why our best course of action is to keep threatening her with what we can tell Hayley – keep the police out of it, at least to start with.'

'I don't care how we get it,' he replies. 'As long as we get some decent money out of her. She'll have had *thousands* from that insurance claim.'

'Shall we try this place? At least we know it's near the bus station.' The bus pulls away leaving us in a cloud of smog.

My feet slide inside my sandals and my jeans feel like they're sticking to me as I hoist my holdall onto my back. I can't recall the last time I bought anything new for myself, therefore, once we've got some money out of Debra, I'm going to treat myself. After all, Turkey is renowned for its genuine fakes. I'll boil to death wearing the clothes I have in my holdall – I didn't realise it would be so hot here. I'm not exactly a seasoned holidaymaker, in fact, I can't remember the last time Pete took me anywhere. It's possibly around eight years ago, as these days, I doubt he'd even walk to the end of the street with me. I look to where Carl's pointing – at a white stone apartment block opposite the market.

'I've just Googled the word on the sign and it means vacancies,' he says.

'Oh, so you've got internet now, have you? Perhaps you should message Debra *again*. I'm sure she'd be interested to know you're here now.'

'Yeah, only since we've got off the bus but it's costing me a fiver per megabyte.' He pulls a face. 'We'll check into that place if we can and then I'll message her. They must have wifi.'

'I bet Debra and Hayley are staying somewhere a million times better than this.' I let a long breath out. 'This place won't even have a pool or air conditioning.'

'Perhaps we can upgrade after we've squeezed some money out of her. That's if we manage it.' Carl's been more sceptical than me ever since I decided we were doing this trip. But I have to remain hopeful. The way my life has panned out over the last couple of years, hope is all I have left.

'Oh she will. And I'm sure it can all be done without you ever having to involve your ex. The threat of it should be enough.' I can't believe I never met her. Only at a distance at the funeral. Carl's *never* brought a girlfriend home to meet me and I know he's had them. No doubt because I've become so dowdy and miserable. Perhaps I can't really blame him.

'Hayley shouldn't even be my *ex*. Which is another reason I hate Debra so much. If it wasn't for her...' His voice trails off.

I think back to what Debra said on the train four months ago about what a lucky escape her daughter had had from her waste of space boyfriend and how much she didn't approve of him. I'd have wiped the floor with her, had I known at the time she was talking about my son. I'm only too aware that Carl can be many things but it's not Debra's judgement to make. Who the hell does she think she is?

'I'm sure that if anyone can persuade Debra of the best course of action now we're here, it's you,' I tell him as I hoist my bag further onto my shoulder while we wait to cross the road into the apartment block. 'Blimey, don't they have speed limits around here?'

'She might also need to be reminded that if we're forced to tell Hayley the truth, I'll *personally* be only too happy to provide a shoulder for Hayley to cry on afterwards.'

His face is hard to read but I get the impression he still carries quite a torch for Hayley. I also get the impression he could have been in touch with her.

Neither is a good thing.

10

DEBRA

'You've been quiet this afternoon.' I nudge Hayley as we walk away from the beach bar and head into the throng of people in the mall. It's safer than walking past Dolphini Village. I still haven't seen Jay since this morning but there's every chance Chantelle could leave there at the same time as us and I'm certain she'd recognise me. Jay might have said something to her by now.

'I'm missing Lance and Dad, to be honest.' Hayley drags her feet as she walks at the side of me. 'I know things had gone wrong for you and Dad but—'

'He was still your dad.' I rub the top of her arm which is slick with suncream. 'And yes, it certainly feels strange for it just to be the two of us away together.'

'It wasn't all bad, was it, Mum? We did have some good times – as a family?'

'Of course we did.' I can't ever expect Hayley to understand how bored I was with her father. We'd got into such a rut and even if Jay hadn't come along, I doubt we'd have lasted much longer.

'I just wish I could stop feeling bad.' Her eyes are glassy with tears as I glance at her. 'We're here in this amazing place,' – she stops and stretches her arms out, – 'while Dad's...' Her words fade away.

'You've got absolutely *nothing* to feel bad about, love. Come here.' I swap my bag onto my other shoulder and sling my arm around her as we continue walking. Her guilt only serves to intensify *mine*. At times like this, I wonder how I can continue living with it. I'm certain it's the reason for my repeated nights of insomnia. Along with the dratted menopause, of course.

'And Lance is all alone at uni.'

'He's not *all alone*. He's got his friends and no doubt he'll be constantly on the phone to Sophie.'

'I guess so.' She sniffs. 'I wish I wasn't single. If only Carl—'

'Surely you don't need me to remind you how much better off you are without him?' I give her a sideward glance. She does seem to have mellowed where he's concerned and could barely contain her disappointment when he came and went at Bryn's funeral. When we got to the wake, she kept watching the door.

'I know.'

'Look, we'll give your brother a call when we get to the hotel if it'll make you feel better. Honestly,' – I nudge her, hoping to distract her attention well away from all thoughts of Carl – 'he'll be far more looking forward to that holiday he's planned with Sophie than he would have done if he'd come away with *us*.'

'I'm just so glad they're back together.'

'She's good for him, isn't she?'

She gives me a funny look. 'Unlike Carl was for me, you mean? You never resist a chance to have a dig.'

'I didn't mean to—'

'Carl wasn't all bad either, you know – especially not in the beginning.'

'They never are to start with.' Here speaks the voice of experience. 'But they show you their true colours in the end, don't they?' I say the second sentence more to myself than to Hayley.

Don't say she's starting to look back at Carl through rose-tinted glasses. Time away from the usual routine and too much time to think can have an odd effect on a person. I had to catch myself when I first saw Jay this morning. I just hope I can sort this latest spiderweb of a situation I'm tangled in before Hayley finds out exactly how close Carl is to us right now.

With him in mind, I swing around to investigate the feeling I've had since first leaving the beach bar – a feeling that someone's following me. But all I see is swarms of people, all clutching bottles of water as they saunter around in the baking heat. I'm certain I'm just being paranoid, at least, I hope I am.

'What's up, Mum?'

'Oh nothing. I er, thought I could have dropped something – I was just checking.'

If Carl had seen us out and about, I'm sure he'd make me aware. He's far too close for comfort, as I found out from his latest message. He threatened that he was coming to Bodrum, but I still can't believe he's actually *here*. I've read the message so many times over the last hour, each word is imprinted on my mind.

> I'm here in Turkey – at the white apartments opposite the bus station - number 21. You have until 10 pm to come round and sort this before I contact Hayley.

Somehow, I've got to get away from Hayley again, this time to go and see Carl. He's the very last person I want her to bump into, especially after what she's just been saying, but mainly for what he's threatening to tell her. She can't ever find out what I did, neither of my kids can. They'd disown me forever and they'd be well within their rights to.

For now, the only thing I can do is be honest with Carl, *and* Tina if she messages again. I'll have to tell them that the insurance money from the pub has failed to materialise, but that I'm here to somehow get as much of my money as I can back from Jay. It seems that I've ignored them for as long as I can get away with.

I honestly thought Tina was a decent sort when I first encoun-tered her on that train – she even bought me a drink. But now, it seems, she's blinded by the possibility of easy money and isn't going to let me go.

'Shall we just have a quiet evening at the hotel tonight?' I say as we weave in and out of the shopkeepers again, ignoring their pleas to explore their wares more closely. I can tell how down in the dumps Hayley must be feeling, not to be dragging me into each and every shop as we make our way past them all. 'The restaurant at the hotel looks lovely,' I add. What I'm thinking is if we're back there, perhaps she'll fall asleep after a few wines – early enough for me to sneak back out to where Carl says he's staying.

'Yeah, that sounds like a plan.' She seems to brighten slightly, evidently buoyed at the prospect of a chilled-out evening.

'Well this is nice, isn't it?' I smile across the table at my daughter, who as always, looks effortlessly beautiful. She's wearing a short blue dress which brings out her eye colour and her blonde hair hangs in waves around her shoulders. I can't get what she said before about missing Lance and Bryn out of my mind and the guilt is almost intolerable. Somehow I've got to get a grip on myself and not allow it to devour me.

I attempt to focus my attention on the crickets which are out in full force as the day fades away, so loud, they're almost drowning out the gentle music that floats from the speakers at each corner of the dining area. I raise my eyes to the tree we're sitting beneath. 'I'd love to get some of those lanterns for the garden at home,' I say.

Hayley's face falls. After all, I don't have a home anymore – there's no longer a garden to hang an ornate candlelit lantern or anything else for that matter. Time to change the subject. 'Have you decided what you're having as your main course, love?' I swirl the wine around in my glass before taking a big sip.

'There's too much choice.' She smiles as she studies the menu, her brows knitted in concentration while my attention is drawn to my phone as it lights up on the table. I don't believe this – it's none other than bloody Carl. I thought he was giving me until 10pm.

> I'm in the lane outside your hotel. I want to speak to you.

Oh no! How the hell does *he* know where we are? I glance at Hayley, thankfully still immersed in the menu. If she'd been looking at me, I'm sure my face would have just given me away.

'I'm torn between the salmon and the chicken. But you know what I'm like, Mum – I'll order something and then when it comes, I'll wish I'd ordered something else. Or I'll be after *yours*.' She laughs then – for the first time in hours. While she continues studying the menu, I tap my screen to open Facebook. I need to know how Carl's discovered where we're staying.

Hayley Ford is with Debra Ford at Su Hotel, Bodrum. She's taken a close-up selfie, showing off the colour in her cheeks which the sun has bestowed. Many of her friends have commented how lovely she looks but unfortunately, they don't seem to be the only ones who've spotted her post. Like me, she doesn't appear to have her settings locked up.

'Order the salmon for me, would you, love? I'll be back in a few minutes.' I drop my phone into my bag and rise from the table.

'Where are you going?'

'I'm just nipping to the loo.' Then as she returns her attention to her menu, I dart in the opposite direction to our hotel room and off towards the main entrance.

I have to get to him before he gets to us.

11

DEBRA

'WHAT THE HELL are *you* doing here?' I hiss at Carl as I approach him out in the lane.

He's leaning up against the wall, all brooding eyes and chiselled jaw. It's easy to see what my daughter saw in him physically. Emotionally, well, he was clearly of the *treat em mean, keep em keen* brigade. I'd have fallen for him too, when I was a girl. Not that I'm any better as a middle-aged woman.

'Like I said, I want a word.'

'Down there, if you don't mind.' I point towards an adjacent street. If Hayley comes looking for me, she'll just check up and down the main lane – I don't think she'd trouble herself with the side streets. I need to get rid of him – and quickly.

'Well you've certainly taken your stalkerish tendencies to a whole new level.' I pause outside a shop where at least there's someone around in case anything gets out of hand here. Carl stops and turns to face me.

'You left me little choice – you haven't even had the decency to reply to any of the messages we've sent.' He steps closer to me.

'I can't *believe* you followed us out here.' I fold my arms to create more of a barrier.

'What else was I supposed to do – other than to confront you face to face?'

'Who the hell do you think you are? You have *no* right coming after us like this.'

A couple who are passing by eye us curiously at my raised voice. They might think we're a couple.

'I've got every right – you owe me.' He surveys me with his steely grey eyes as he waits for my response.

'I haven't got anything to give you.' My voice wobbles. How am I ever going to get them off my back?

'Five grand and a third of the insurance money – those were my terms when I set it all up with Bryn. Yet so far, I've not received a penny.'

'There *is* no insurance money.' Perhaps if there was, I *would* throw something their way. Anything so I wouldn't have to hear from them again.

'Try again, Debra. We don't believe you.'

'As I already told your mother at Bryn's funeral, Jay took off with *everything* I've got.'

'That doesn't make any sense. *He's taken off with everything you've got,*' – he mimics my voice so venomously I feel like slapping him. 'If that's the case, how come you and Hayley are here on some luxury holiday?'

'I've come after him.'

'You've found him then?' Suddenly his whole demeanor changes.

'He's in the process of buying into a beach bar.'

'So you've *spoken*?'

'Of course we have. I've told him I want my money back or I'm...' My words fade out. Bloody hell – why I am I telling Carl any of this? He's the last person I should explain myself to. He'll use anything I say as ammunition. He might even be recording me like I recorded Jay.

'I know it was *Jay* who started the fire.' Carl cocks his head to one side as he awaits my reaction, his gelled hair glistening in the overhead street light. It's nearly dark now but not as dark as I feel inside.

I stare back at him. He can't possibly know this. I didn't even know Jay was going to become involved when I spoke to Tina. When I spilled my guts to her, I hadn't got that far with my plan. All I knew was I was going to find out who Bryn had employed for the 'job' and offer whoever it was more money to do things my way. But with Jay stepping in, it never came to that.

'Jay was running away from the pub as I got there.' Carl maintains his gaze with me. 'Just as the fire was taking hold in the staff room. So perhaps you should be letting *me* know where he is.'

'I'm not joining forces with *you*.' I spit the word *you* out like it's something poisonous. As it is.

'Who said anything about joining forces?' His top lip curls into a sneer.

As well as the leverage Carl's got over me, perhaps he's going to go for double bubble and try holding Jay to ransom as well. If he finds him, that is.

'Nor am I going to allow you,' I continue. 'or your mother to keep blackmailing me.'

'I don't care for the word, *blackmail*.' He steps closer. 'I prefer the word insurance.'

'Insurance?' My voice is almost a squeak. How could Hayley have possibly said to me, *he wasn't all bad, Mum*? Clearly her instincts where men are concerned are as shaky as mine.

'At the moment Hayley believes her father set that fire going himself, doesn't she?'

'That was his original plan – as you very well know.' I throw my arms in the air. 'Jay would have died in there if Bryn had had his way.'

I wish I'd never overheard Bryn on the phone and never known about his plans to end my affair by getting rid of Jay, who went and left me anyway. I've never been more duped by anyone.

'You still haven't said why you're here, stalking us like this.'

'Me and Hayley have been messaging since the funeral,' he says, as if that's supposed to explain things.

I knew it. Something twists in my stomach. Surely Hayley would have mentioned something to *me*. 'I don't believe you, Carl. She wouldn't be so stupid after how you treated her last year.'

'You've never liked me, have you?' He hooks his thumbs into the waistband of his shorts. 'You've always treated me like I'm something you stepped in.'

I stand up tall. He's *not* going to intimidate me. 'You were a shit to my daughter, Carl. What do you expect?'

'A bit more respect at this moment, actually. You need to remember who's calling the shots here.' His voice is more pleasant than the expression on his face.

'You can call as many shots as you want – I can't give you what I haven't got.' I shrug.

'Well, I suggest you try a bit harder then. I'm not leaving this place without my money.'

'*Your* money – there *is* no money, and besides, it's not even *my* debt.' I throw my arms in the air. 'How many times?'

'It's your debt *now*. And I'm not going away.'

I drop my arms down by my sides. I need to get rid of him. 'Look, I've given Jay twenty-four hours to get back to me.' I shouldn't be telling Carl anything but I just need him off my back, if only just for tonight so I can get back to Hayley. I've no idea what I'm to tell her about where I've been. She'll have checked the hotel room for me by now so I'll have to think of something good.

'The moment you hear from him, you let me know, do you understand?'

'I've said I will, haven't I?' I step around him.

'Because if you don't get me our money.' He steps to the side, blocking my path. 'Make no bones about it...'

'What?' I grit my teeth.

'It won't be you I message for a chat next time I turn up here. It'll be Hayley. And I'll tell her *everything*.'

'She wouldn't believe you anyway.' I hold eye contact with him.

'Do you really want to take that chance?'

He's right. Even if Carl's version of events only starts to sow the *seeds* of doubt in her mind, she'll keep pushing until she gets to the truth. That's what she's like – never satisfied until she knows all there is to know about *anything*.

'And guess who's shoulder she'll be crying on?' Carl continues with a sneer. 'Chances are it won't be yours.'

12

DEBRA

'WHERE THE HELL have you been, Mum? I've searched *everywhere* for you?' Hayley looks panic-stricken as she rushes towards me. The call to prayer echoes out into the evening, making things seem more unreal than they already are.

'I'm really sorry, love.' Think fast, think fast. 'I just needed some air.'

'What are you talking about? We were already sitting outside.'

I glance over at a couple sitting at a table on the edge of the dining area watching our altercation, possibly wondering what on earth there could be to row about in such a beautiful place.

'Keep your voice down, Hayley. We don't want everyone to know our business. I was having one of my anxiety attacks if you must know. I needed to get out of here for a few minutes.'

'Why didn't you say something then?' Her voice is gentler now.

'I just needed to get away – and I didn't want to worry you. I'm sorry.' I reach for her arm. 'I'm OK now – it's just because we're here – in a strange place and all that.'

'Well I was really worried there, Mum.' Her face falls. 'I couldn't bear to lose you. It brought it all back for a few minutes.'

I know exactly what she's referring to. Once again, the night when I put Jay before my own children is coming back to haunt me. At least Carl doesn't know about any of *that*. Unless Hayley's ever chosen to tell him. Another reason I've got to keep the two of them apart.

'Look I'm back now and like I said, I'm really sorry, I just had a funny moment. Let's eat, shall we? I don't know about you but I could do with an early night.'

'They've already brought our food.' She gestures towards the table. 'It should still be warm.'

'I could do with another glass of wine first.'

At least I don't need to leave here to visit Carl's apartment now. If Hayley was to wake and find me gone, she'd have a meltdown.

But if Jay hasn't got in touch with me by lunchtime tomorrow, I'll have to get away to pay him another little visit.

I wake with the smell of burning in my nostrils and smoke choking me. I'm struggling to get any breath in and my chest feels as though it might explode. I can't see anything through the smoke but then realise that's not the only thing preventing me from getting any air in, it's also Bryn's stranglehold around my neck. I dig my nails into the flesh of his fingers – if I don't get him off me within the next thirty seconds or so, I'm done for.

I sit up with a start, drenched in sweat and gulping air in as I try to get myself back together. I'm safe. Bryn's dead and I'm here with Hayley. Much as I don't want to, I've been dreaming about the fire again.

It's 3am. Wine knocks me out each night, enabling me to get straight off to sleep but then it's as though my internal body clock is set for 3am, even with the time difference here in Turkey. It's a punishing time, the hours I lie awake each night until dawn, but perhaps it's all I deserve. Me, alone with my conscience and the darkness.

I point the remote up at the air conditioning unit. As I reach for my water, Carl's visit and everything he said, particularly his threat to go to Hayley if I don't pay up, floods my brain again. Shit. Shit. Shit. I feel like repeatedly throwing my head against the pillow. Doesn't he and Tina realise how powerless I am? Apart from a few thousand pounds which my father left behind, I've got nothing to speak of. And they're not getting *that*.

I glance across at my daughter's sleeping form. I used to sleep soundly like that. I'd snuggle into Bryn in our early days and be asleep within moments. Then I wouldn't wake until the next morning. I sometimes wonder how long I'll be able to go on like this. If it's not my menopausal body calling the shots each night, it's my muddled mind.

Flicking my phone onto Facebook, I once again find myself on the page of Chantelle Wilson. There she is, leaning into Jay on the deck of what must be the Bodrum Belle. Bronzed and beautiful, she looks like she doesn't have a care in the world. I hate her. And as for him – he certainly doesn't look troubled by the visit I paid him. I wonder if he's even given my ultimatum a second thought.

It's no good. I can't lie here a second longer. I need to do what I came here to do and I need to sort it before Hayley wakes up. It's not even seven yet and judging from the amount of wine we both put away last night, she should be out for the count for at least another couple of hours. She always is when we're at home.

Swinging my legs out of bed, I tiptoe to my still-packed suitcase and take a fresh dress and cardigan from the top before creeping into the bathroom to get dressed. Then silently sliding a bottle of water from the fridge, I head towards the door, stealing a quick look back at my still-sleeping daughter before clicking it closed behind me.

The pool looks inviting in the stillness of the early morning, bathed in the soft glow of dawn. I'd love to jump in and swim away my troubles, but instead, I walk around its perimeter and head over the crazy paving towards the exit.

I can walk down the centre of the lane outside, all the crazy moped riders and indignant Turkish taxi drivers are still evidently asleep. So are several dogs in doorways. One or two open their eyes as I pass and my heart breaks for them. I must get back to the collection box which was labelled *food for strays* and leave some money. I'd come back and open a sanctuary for them all if I could. I'm in this beautiful place but I just want to get back to my own dog now. Back to Yorkshire, where somehow, I've got to get rid of the ghosts that are haunting me once and for all and start rebuilding my life.

All the shops are closed and there's barely a soul in sight as I continue down towards the harbour. I stand for a few moments, staring out at the sun as it begins lighting up the water. Just for a minute, my mood lifts with it as I realise really, how insignificant both me and my problems are in the magnitude of the still-turning earth. My life might have been on pause for the last few months but for everyone else and for nature itself, it all moves on. I've just got to make sure I'm not left behind.

Then I remember with a feeling of sickness that Bryn's life doesn't go on. Instead, I came right down to his level to deal with him – no, in fact, I sank lower.

I trudge on, past boat after silent boat. What a way of life this must be. *These* people are living, rather than just existing – a sharp reminder of how the weeks, months and years are passing me by. I've spent my entire adult life either shackled to a man or blinded by the promises of one. It's time to stand up and be counted. Just me, finally standing on my own.

Eventually, I reach the Bodrum Belle, her doors closed and her shutters pulled down. A wind chime tinkles in the breeze as she rocks gently on the water. I imagine Jay shacked up with Chantelle in there, tucked in behind her like he was with me on the all-too-brief night we spent together. He'll be lulled in his untroubled sleep by the motion of the boat.

My internal world was, for a moment, calm but at the reminder of his betrayal, it once again catches fire.

'Open up.' I thump at the door of the boat. 'I want to talk to you, Jay.'

13

DEBRA

'WHAT THE—' Jay throws the door open. The sight of him in his boxers with sleep-tousled hair evokes tears that stab at my eyes. He's living *our* dream – the one I'd have given my heart and soul to share with him. Only he's sharing it with *her*. 'Oh, it's you. How did you know where I was?'

I blink away my tears and stand with my hands on my hips. 'Your so-called business partner told me.'

Jay shrugs a t-shirt over his head as he glances back into the boat before stepping out onto the deck, pulling the door after him. 'What do you even want?'

I can't believe he's asking me this. 'You *know* what I want. Especially since I haven't had a word out of you since yesterday.'

'So you come banging me up at this hour?' He points along the row of boats. 'It's a wonder you haven't woken the entire harbour.'

'All I care about is getting my fifty grand.' I fold my arms as I fix my eyes on his, while squinting in the peachy-pink sunrise behind him. Once I'd have dreamed about watching the sun come up with him at my side. I can hardly believe how it's all turned out.

He shuffles to the end of the decking in bare feet and steps off onto the concrete, now facing me. Even his feet are perfect.

'It's not as simple as you think – like I've told you – I've sunk my money into that beach bar – I'm not entirely sure what you want me to do.'

'It's not *your* money, though, is it?'

'Some of it is. Look, I just need a little longer to—'

'It's all still subject to contract – I've checked it out.' I square up to him, hopefully portraying that I mean business here. 'Which means the money hasn't even left your account yet.'

'I've signed on the dotted line, Deb.'

'Don't *Deb* me. I want it back, Jay, and I meant what I said about going to the police. I can have you extradited back to the UK.'

'Even though you'll be implicating yourself?' He cocks his head to one side, his eyes darkening. 'Because rest assured, if you try dragging me down that road, I'll be dragging you right down with me. Plus I'll be putting *all* the blame onto *you*.'

'*You* lit the match.'

'*You* locked him in there.' His jaw hardens. 'Plus you gave me the nod of when to go.'

'You were the one who came up with it all.' A memory of him roaring up on his motorbike to meet me on the morning of New Year's Day fills my mind – after he'd planned everything to the letter. If only I'd kept our messages from around that time. Not that he could know I haven't. 'And I can prove it.'

'You still allowed it to happen. Which makes you as guilty as I am. So do your worst, Deb.' He throws his arms into the air. 'Fuck *both* our lives up if you want.'

'I've just about lost everything anyway. All I have left are my kids.'

'Aren't they enough for you?' He gives me a look I've never seen from him before. One which hovers somewhere between pity and irritation. 'You bleated on enough about how you couldn't bear to leave them behind.'

'I wouldn't expect *you* to understand. All you care about is yourself.'

'I'm just not as pathetic as you are.' He leans against the railing. 'So do yourself a favour and just go back to them.' He shakes his head. 'I never thought I'd have to hear about them again. I had enough when that meddling daughter of yours summoned me to her house on New Year's Day.'

'What do you mean?' My indignation gives way to shock. Why has Hayley never mentioned this?

'Like mother–like daughter, that's all I can say.' His face is thin and pinched. 'Giving me ultimatums, she was. Acting as entitled as you do.'

There'll be time soon to confront Hayley with this. When I can decide on the best way of approaching it. For now, however, I need to focus on being repaid.

'I'm just entitled to the money you so callously robbed from me.'

'No can do, Deb.' He pulls a face – a cross between apology and nonchalance. 'You need to walk away from this.'

'So you're not going to give it back then. *Any* of it?' My voice rises. 'So you were lying when you said you needed time?' Of course he was. I should have carried out my threat yesterday when his precious beach bar was full of customers, instead of giving him the benefit of the doubt.

He shrugs again. 'I've already made an agreement for the beach bar. Like I keep telling you.'

'And you made an agreement with *me*.' I point at myself. 'Don't push me here, Jay. I mean every word I'm saying about what I'll do.'

'What the hell's going on out here?' Chantelle pokes her head out of the door. 'Oh, it's *you*.' Her gaze shifts from me to Jay as she tucks her hair behind her ears. 'I thought you said you were getting rid of her.' Her eyes are still rimmed with last night's mascara.

'Getting *rid* of me?' I turn back to Jay. 'And how do you propose you're going to do that?'

He looks down at his feet. 'You need to go quietly, Deb,' he says.

'*Deb*?' Chantelle's voice has a mocking edge.

'We know people here now.' Jay keeps his attention fixed on me. 'People who we only need to say the word to.'

'What word? Hang on – are you threatening me?'

'You're nothing but a dried-up old has-been.' Chantelle smirks. 'How did you ever think he'd be interested in *you*?' She throws her head back in laughter.

'Were you in on all this together from the start?' I step towards her. 'How much do you know?'

'Just leave us alone.' Jay steps forward and grabs my arm, his tone bearing even more caution. At a guess, I'd say she knows about the money side of things and that he duped me into thinking we were running away together. I bet she knows nothing of his involvement with Bryn's death.

'Did you both target me all along?' I shake my arm free and look from him to her. 'I want to know.'

'Just go, will you?'

The door on the boat next to us bangs against a railing as it's thrown open and a Turk in boxer shorts steps out onto the deck, flinging his arms in the air and spouting something in Turkish.

Jay says something back to him and for a moment, I'm almost impressed – I didn't realise he could speak Turkish. Then, with a thud, I remember why I'm here. Nothing about Jay should impress me anymore. Not after how he's treated me.

I feel like dragging Chantelle off this boat by her hair and pushing her into that water. Then holding her head beneath the surface. 'Answer my question then. I want to know if I was targeted all along by you both.' I hate her even more than I hate Carl and Tina for blackmailing me – which is really saying something.

'If you think stalking us is going to get you anywhere, believe me, you'll live to regret it.'

I look back at Jay.

'You can come round here shooting your mouth off all you want,' he says, 'but we both know you're unlikely to get anywhere with your threats, don't we?'

'You haven't heard the last of me.' I stumble away from them, blinking back tears. At least I know the score now. He lied to me yesterday to avoid me informing his prospective business partner and customers about the real him.

But he won't stop me today.

~

Hayley's in tears when I arrive back at our room.

'Hey, what's the matter?' I rush to her bed, guilt almost forcing the air from my lungs. 'I woke early and just went for a walk. I haven't even been that long.' I glance at my watch.

'I had a dream that Dad was still alive.' She sobs as she hugs her knees to her chest. 'It was so real. I keep having the same dream and then when I wake up and remember he's gone— It's awful Mum – I just can't bear it.'

I pull her towards me as she sobs, wanting to tell her about my recurring dream but really, I don't deserve any sympathy. 'There, there,' I rock her in my arms, like I did when she was small as the air conditioning cools me. 'I'm here now, and everything's going to be OK.' I kiss the top of her head, feeling even more protective of her than normal, especially now I know Carl's hanging around like a noxious substance.

Only everything's *not* going to be OK. Jay's *not* going to pay me anything back and both Carl and his mother are *never* going to leave me alone. My only option is starting to look like just returning home and handing over every penny of Dad's meagre inheritance to them. That's if they'd even accept an amount far less than what they're demanding.

'Look, we'll have a lovely day together today.' I inhale the scent of Hayley's hair as I try to force some positivity into my voice. 'How about going back to where we were yesterday for lunch and then we'll have a visit to the Turkish Baths like you wanted? If that doesn't relax us both, I don't know what will.'

I also need to keep her well out of Carl's way.

'Come on then.' I let her go and give her a gentle nudge. 'Let's get some breakfast and get ourselves out of here before the best spots on that beach get taken.'

'Can I ask you about something?' I look up from buttering my toast. I've got to ask her about what Jay mentioned – it's going to drive me nuts until I know what they were talking about.

Hayley pauses from spooning cereal into her mouth. 'Sure, what?'

'Did Jay come to see you on New Year's Day?'

She puts her spoon down slowly. 'How do you know about *that*? Did Lance tell you?'

'He must have done,' I reply, knowing I need to choose my words carefully. So Lance knew as well. I'd have thought *he'd* have mentioned something. 'I'd forgotten all about it, to be honest, but then something must have jogged my memory while I was out for my walk this morning.'

'I just asked him to come round.' She fiddles with the corner of her napkin. 'For all the good it did.' Her eyes fill with sadness and she bites her lip.

'But why?' I'm now wondering if Hayley could have said something to Jay that caused him to have a change of heart with me. Perhaps he *wasn't* stringing me along the whole time. I nibble at my toast as I wait for her answer. My appetite's totally left me.

'Dad phoned me on New Year's Day morning.' She stares down at her hands. 'He was distraught, Mum. I had to do *something* to try and change things. Plus, call us selfish but Lance and I didn't want you to run off with *Jay* either.'

'And what did he say to you?'

'Who? Jay? Well pardon my French but he was a complete prick. Said you were a grown woman and then something about not having to wipe our arses anymore.' Her tone hardens. 'It should have been *him* they pulled out of the pub, not Dad.'

I swallow my tea. Yes, it *should* have been Jay. And all because of me, it wasn't. And if I'd had any sense about me, I could have called a halt to the whole thing and it wouldn't have been *anyone*. I've wished so many times I could turn the clock back.

'How come you never mentioned it to me before?'

'It didn't seem important and sort of paled into insignificance after what happened to Dad.' She picks her spoon back up. 'Anyway, can we talk about something else?' She looks around at the other tables, all filled with people having what sounds like normal, pleasant conversation. 'We're supposed to be on holiday.'

14

DEBRA

I LAY my book face down on the table. I've been staring at the same paragraph for over ten minutes without taking in a word of it. How can I focus on a story with all this turmoil swirling around in my head? I need to make a decision. I could cut my losses as far as Jay's concerned, try to enjoy the rest of my week with Hayley then go home, *or* continue to fight for what's mine.

With Carl circling like a vulture, I don't think I've got much choice in the matter. He doesn't seem to believe that I've got nothing left. I honestly don't think he'll ever leave me alone and even if I manage to pay him off, who's to say he won't be back for more?

We're in the same spots we were in yesterday, so I can also keep Jay's beach bar in my line of vision. The last time I went for a swim, Chantelle was lounging around again like the Queen of Sheba, and Jay was laughing with his business partner. They don't give a shit about me – they've taken what they wanted and are now expecting me to crawl back under my stone.

We've had lunch, or should I say, I've picked at a sandwich and

I'm onto my second glass of wine which has thankfully, gone some way towards settling my frazzled nerves. But I still keep expecting Carl to jump out from behind one of the sunbeds. I feel like I'm being watched the entire time. It's awful. At least Hayley hasn't tagged us on Facebook today so he won't come looking here.

'I'm going for a wander, Mum.' Hayley sits up on her lounger and stretches down to reach her sandals. 'I fancy a look around the shops.'

'Oh erm, wouldn't you rather stay here? Are you not having a nice time?' The prospect of her wandering around and bumping into Carl or Jay isn't a good one.

She gives me a strange look. 'I want to stretch my legs. Are you coming?'

'Why don't we have a look around later?' By then, I'll persuade her into something else. We risk bumping into Carl every time we leave the hotel, without opening ourselves up further.

'Because I want to go *now.*'

'You said you wanted to spend the day *here*?'

'Am I not allowed to change my mind? We're on holiday, aren't we?'

'OK, OK, but do you mind if I stay here? Besides...' I glance behind us. 'It's filling up – we don't want to lose our places, do we?'

She twists her hair into a bun at the top of her head. 'I'll be fine on my own. Do you want anything?'

I shake my head. 'I'll just be here, carrying on with my book.'

I turn in my seat and watch as she walks away. I can only hope and pray she doesn't bump into either of them, especially while I'm not with her. But there are so many people around that with a bit of luck, she'll just blend into the crowd.

I lean back on my lounger and gaze out to sea. Everyone's happy and relaxed as they float on lilos, chasing each other around or snorkelling in the water. Exactly as they should be when somewhere this amazing.

Meanwhile, I'm as miserable as a wet weekend in Scarborough

and my insides are churning like a cement mixer. I've never felt so stressed in all my life. If it's not my previous wrongdoing troubling me, it's my lack of financial stability and not having my own roof over my head any more. Or it's loneliness, or the fact that I'm being blackmailed.

And I have only *one* way of resolving several of these problems.

I've got the chance to act while Hayley's out of the way. I swing my legs around on my lounger and stand from it, ensuring I leave our towels to secure our places with my book face down on mine and a bottle of suncream and Hayley's magazine on hers. It's now or never.

'We're coming back.' I gesture to the woman next to me. I've heard her speaking in French to the woman she's with so I'm unsure if she knows what I'm saying as I point from my place to Hayley's. 'Can you watch?' I point from my eyes to our things.

She nods, seemingly understanding me, so I slide my feet into my flip-flops. Then, throwing my bag over my shoulder, I thread my way between the loungers and back onto the pebbles towards the exit.

'You leave?' Says the proprietor. 'You pay bill?'

'I'll be back in five minutes,' I tell him. I spread out my fingers, then point at my watch. 'We stay all afternoon.' I gesture back towards our places. 'I just need to see someone.'

'OK,' he replies. I must look like a respectable sort of person for he lets me go. Perhaps he thinks Hayley's still sitting over there if he didn't see her leave a few minutes ago.

My heart's hammering as I get closer and closer to Dolphini Village. What I'm about to do won't achieve anything but it's better than going quietly and 'crawling back under my stone.' Jay and Chantelle need to see that I'm prepared to put up a fight to get what's rightly mine. His threats about 'knowing people' are just a load of crap. He's only been in Bodrum for five minutes. What 'people' could he possibly know who would do something bad to a middle-aged English woman who's only trying to recoup her stolen money?

'Hello again.' I sidle up to the man I spoke to yesterday. The one who told me where Jay was staying.

'Ah, you're Jay's friend. I get him for you.' He points to the front row of the sun loungers.

'No – it's *you* I came to speak to.' I glance over to where Jay's sitting beside Chantelle, laughing with her like he hasn't got a care in the world.

The man looks puzzled. 'But he's just there.' He gestures towards the back of his head.

'The thing is, before you get into business with him, you should know that he's a thief. A lying, cheating thief. You really shouldn't trust him. He'll rip you off, he'll take all your money.'

'Who are you?' The man frowns. 'Jayden, come.' He raises his voice.

'Please listen to me,' I plead. 'I employed him as my bar manager and trusted him with the safe, with the login for my bank account. He stole the lot from me – everything.'

'Jayden.' His voice rises higher,

Jay twists in his seat, frowning at first, then on seeing me, he jumps to his feet. 'I told *you* to stay away.' He wags his finger in my direction.

'He'll do the same to you,' I continue. 'You should pull out of your *business deal* while you still can. He's not to be trusted.'

The beach bar is packed as Jay darts towards me. 'This man killed my husband,' I shout and everyone turns around. 'He locked him inside a building, then set fire to it.' There are puzzled stares but several people must be able to understand me as they turn to look at Jay. 'And he's taken all our money,' I continue, suddenly taken aback as the memory of Bryn standing on the bar of The

Dales Inn, proclaiming his *watch this space* threats to anyone who'd listen, fill my mind. I'm acting exactly the same as he did. 'Find somewhere else to spend your day,' I yell. 'Don't give your money to this *murderer*.' I'm hysterical as Jay grabs me from behind and claps his hand over my mouth.

'You mad bitch,' he bellows as he marches me backwards and rams me up against the wall of the building. 'Is this the best you've got? Most of the people here can't understand a word of English anyway.'

Chantelle saunters over to us, tossing her mane of hair behind one shoulder. 'I see you've done a great job of getting rid of her, Jay.' She shakes her head. 'Must try harder.'

15

DEBRA

'Is this the place you were talking about?' I point at the sign saying Turkish Baths.

'Yeah, it's supposed to be most effective for your tan when you have one at the start and then at the end of your holiday.'

It's on the tip of my tongue to tell her that this isn't a holiday for me and that I don't give a rat's arse about getting a tan, but I've got to keep walking the walk for her sake. She hasn't a clue that anything's untoward and somehow, I plan to keep it that way. She enjoyed a wander around the shops, bought herself a couple of tops and then returned to find me in exactly the same place she left me in. So far, she's none the wiser about what I'm really up to in Bodrum.

I must admit that a Turkish bath will do me the world of good. I don't think my neck could be any more sore after craning it to my right-hand side all day to keep tabs on Jay and Chantelle. I haven't laid eyes on him again this afternoon after he gloriously frog-marched me from Dolphini Village, but *she's* barely moved a muscle every time I've swum back over to the green umbrellas. I've made no effort to conceal myself amongst the other swimmers when I've swum over this time. I've nothing to lose anymore.

As Hayley tries to make out the times and prices, I glance around to make sure no one's followed us. After all Jay's threats, not to mention Carl's, I really don't feel safe.

I follow my daughter into the cooler building and let her do the talking when we reach the desk. I'm going to force myself to relax for the next hour or so, and somehow attempt to chase all the crap from my mind. The man at reception swipes Hayley's card and begins to lead me in one direction whilst gesturing to another man to lead her in another, as if it's the done thing for women to be separated and go off to opposite ends of the building with strange men.

'Actually, can we stay together?' Hayley echoes my fears – and with a look which suggests it could be the last time we'll ever see each other again. I have to admit that I thought we'd be seen by female staff at a place like this. Perhaps we should have booked a Turkish Baths in advance – rather than just walking in here off the street like we have.

'Women inside.' The man points at a door.

'It'll be fine,' I reassure her. 'I'll be waiting right here when we've done. You go and just relax.' But as she heads off down the corridor, looking back at me again before she disappears through a door, I almost have second thoughts. Suddenly, it takes all I've got not to go after her. After all, she's only twenty-three, we're in a foreign country and I've let her be led away by some man who could be capable of anything, even if he has assured us there'll be a woman actually doing Hayley's treatment. But then I give myself a shake. I'm getting as worrisome as she is. But it's no wonder after the message I received half an hour ago from Carl. I pull my phone from my bag to see if there's been anything else.

> I'm fast running out of patience. Don't take me for a mug – I meant what I said. Hayley's already messaged today. She'd be surprised if I let her know just how close by I am.

I can't believe she's messaging with him again. I'll have to steer the subject onto him to see if she'll mention anything. No doubt, he'll be turning on the charm while trying to reel her back in, especially while she's been so vulnerable over the last few months. But letting him *anywhere* near her could be the biggest mistake she'll ever make.

'Lift. Turn. Relax.' I wince as a bowl of cold water is thrown over me, but there's no denying that being here has done me the power of good. I thought that nothing could possibly unwind my knotted-up muscles and release the tension headache that's been ever present since the turn of the year but I'm pleased to say that the magic this buxom Turkish woman has yielded has made all the difference.

Having my hair washed by her nearly made me cry. All I could think about was the mother I lost when I was eleven years old. The woman's fingers on my scalp became *her* fingers as I got a flashback to being a girl again.

This whole trip's having a strange effect on me. I'm veering between relaxation and utter anxiety, and then feeling like I *can* get through this before suddenly succumbing to the depths of guilt and despair. And because I'm constantly around Hayley, I'm having to keep a really tight grip on myself. I only hope she's alright through there.

And now for the really wonderful part. The woman gestures for me to lie face down on the slab as she begins to work the warm oil into my back. Again, I want to cry. It's been so long since I've felt another person's hands on my skin, even if we've had to pay a thousand lira each for the privilege. 'Relax,' she orders, for what must be the millionth time since I got here. She must be puzzled by me, this pale and not-so-interesting English woman who's like a coiled spring and has been on the verge of tears since arriving.

I try to let my muscles go. But I'm only too aware that this could now be the calm before the storm. Particularly after my earlier outburst at the Dolphini Village beach bar. Even if, miraculously, I get no backlash from Jay, I've still got that message from Carl to worry about. Perhaps when I check my phone, there'll be another one.

The woman's hands on my head feel wonderful as she kneads her thumbs into the base of my skull and then around to my temples. This is the best headache cure I've ever come across. If only other things could be cured so easily.

My back feels almost in pain after all the kneading and pummelling as I dress again. Is this how it's supposed to feel after a Turkish bath? However, I feel cleaner than I have in a long time though it's a shame the same can't be said for my internal world.

I drag a comb through my matted hair and hope my daughter has managed to relax more than I did. It was, after all, Hayley who was so insistent and excited about us coming here. Until she was led in the other direction, that is. I swap the heat of the changing area for the comparative coolness of the foyer and approach the desk where a different man is sitting behind it now.

'My daughter?' I say as he looks at me quizzically. I glance up and down the corridor. She's probably still getting ready.

He shakes his head but I'm not sure if he's even understood me. I'll just have to wait until she comes out.

There's another message from Carl.

> You've got an hour. If you don't come up with the goods, I'm arranging to meet Hayley.

I check the time of the message. Shit. It must have been sent just as we arrived here – much more than an hour ago.

> I need more time. Jay won't pay up. I'm working out how much I'll be able to give you.

I can hardly believe I'm being blackmailed in this way. Perhaps I'll change my name back to my maiden name when we get back to

England and maybe I'll move away. I'll delete my Facebook profile and stay off grid so no one can find me. The problem is though, Hayley and Lance are so active on social media. The way to get to me is through them – and the way to *hurt* me is through them. Carl clearly knows that.

I keep glancing at my phone as I wait for her to come out. Carl doesn't reply to my message. I send another one – this time, to Hayley.

> I'm waiting for you in reception, love. See you shortly.

That will hurry her along. I wait another ten minutes. It's been half an hour since I left the changing area to wait for her. She's slow at getting ready but not this slow. She hasn't even read my message.

I try ringing her. But her phone's switched off.

16

DEBRA

I TYPE English to Turkish translation into my phone. *Have you seen my daughter?* I stride over to the counter, hold it up to the man and then point along the corridor in the direction she went.

He looks me in the eye, shrugs and then settles back onto his stool. I really don't know what to do but what I do know is that I'm beginning to panic.

I wait another ten minutes. Because she still hasn't read my message, I return to the counter. Maybe it was too hot in there and she's passed out. Maybe she's got herself worked up about something.

The man turns back to his computer.

'Can you go and see if she's alright?' I slap my palm onto the desk. 'Please!' He shrugs again, his gaze calm and passive, so I tear along the corridor.

He bellows something after me.

As I barge into the room at the end, another lady is having a treatment.

'Hayley,' I call out, looking across at the changing area off the room. The curtain isn't drawn and there's absolutely no sign of her.

'My daughter,' I yell, my voice echoing around the stone tiles. 'Where is she?' I'm becoming more and more frantic by the second.

'Back, now.' The man grabs my arm and drags me backwards as he pulls the door closed. His English isn't *that* bad. Surely I can get him to help me find Hayley.

I try to yank my arm from his grip as he frogmarches me back up the corridor. 'Where is she?' I cry. 'She wouldn't have just left without me.'

I break free of him and rush outside. Why the hell didn't I think to check out here for her? She must have decided to get some fresh air and be sitting on a wall, engrossed in her phone.

Only she isn't.

Shit. Maybe she's gone back to the hotel. This doesn't make any sense but I've got to check before I *really* start to panic. Before I set off, I type out another message, to Carl this time. It's the only place I can imagine she'll be. He must have followed us here and taken her off somewhere.

If you're with Hayley, please don't say anything to her. I'm just working out what I can give you. If you tell her anything, you'll get nothing.

I'll lose my children. I can't imagine how they'd react if they knew the truth. And I have no defense, not really. Other than vanity and being flattered at the time.

Tomorrow, I'll call the solicitor and find out exactly what's coming my way from Dad's estate. I'll ask for something in writing – something I can show to buy me the time until it comes through and I can pay Carl off. My children's love and respect are worth far more than any money.

Carl's read my message but he doesn't reply. He'll be trying to make me sweat. However, I don't believe he'll have said anything to Hayley yet – if that's where she is, after all, to do so would take away any power he has over me. So I have to stay positive and I have to remain calm.

I arrive back at our hotel. I've half walked and half ran, ignoring the indignant cries of those I've managed to knock into en route. As I tear past those seated in the outdoor restaurant for the evening, several hotel guests glance up at me, most likely wondering what's up with the barmy English woman this time. I hurtle past the pool and tug at the door to our room. It's locked. With shaking hands, I snatch the key from my bag and unlock the door, knowing before I even open it that she won't have been back.

As I thought, the room's in semi-darkness and all is just as we left it this morning. In a heap of clothes, hairbrushes and make-up. Room service must have been in to make our beds and replenish our coffee. But as for Hayley, there's absolutely no sign.

I open my phone again. *Please, please, please.* There's a message from Carl.

> I'm not with her.

> Are you telling me the truth?

> Why would I lie? You'll be the first to know when I see her.

Oh my God. Where the hell is she?

I try to call her again. Her phone's still switched off. I'm fighting back tears as I race back through the hotel grounds and towards the exit, narrowly missing being hit by a moped as I dash out into the lane.

The rider pauses, yells what is no doubt a Turkish expletive at me, before revving up again and continuing on his way.

'Where the hell are you, Hayley?' I cry out into the now-falling dusk as I start back in the direction of the Turkish Baths. I'll force them to help me this time – there has to be a manager there. If there's still no sign of her by the time I get back, I'll have to call the police.

I'm struggling to get my breath in and I've never known fear like it in my life. If anything's happened to my beautiful daughter, I won't be able to go on.

Then it dawns on me. I'm chasing in the wrong direction, messaging Carl.

After turning up at his boat this morning and then his bar this afternoon, I bet Hayley's disappearance is something to do with Jay.

'You have a photo?'

I bring one up on Facebook that she tagged herself in earlier. Tears pool in my eyes at the sight of her beaming face. I should have protected her to the ends of the earth. If anything happens it will be all my fault. The police officer scans it onto a device.

'And you last saw her go through the door?' The officer points at the spot where I last set eyes on my daughter as I rock myself back and forth in my seat. The man behind the counter at the Turkish Baths is watching our conversation with distaste written all over his face. Evidently, we must be bad for his business.

I gesture to him to give me the use of paper and pen and write down the address where Carl said he's staying and also the name of Jay's boat and the beach bar.

'Not our friends,' I tell him, speaking slowly in order that he might realise the gravity of my words. 'They might have her.'

'She knows them?' He frowns.

I nod then say. 'They don't like me.' I point at myself as I shake my head. 'They could hurt her to hurt me.'

He looks confused.

'Please, please just find her.' My voice is bordering on hysteria as I stand from the bench and pace the stone floor. I can't take much more. They have to find her. I don't know what I'll do if they don't.

'She's been gone, for how long?' The other officer asks.

'I haven't seen her for nearly three hours.' I pause in front of him. I'll have to let Lance know soon if they don't find her with any of the details I've given them. I honestly think that Jay's carried out the threat he made this morning. *I know people,* he said. And he certainly looked angry enough this afternoon.

'She's young and pretty and I'm terrified she's going to get hurt.'

Another officer is outside on his radio. Hayley's name is mentioned. At last, they're actually doing something.

'Why couldn't they have taken *me?*' I can't hold back the tears any longer. 'How the hell have I allowed this to happen?'

The two officers still in the same room as me look baffled.

'Wait at Su Otel,' the first officer says. 'If she returns, inform us straight away.'

I nod, the lump in my throat so huge, I can't speak.

I'm sobbing as I dash back out into the night. I don't know what to do and everyone's looking at me. As I reach the first junction, I pause for a moment to get myself back together. I load up Messenger as I walk along the road, the noise of people enjoying themselves in the bars which line the street ringing out into the night. I can cope with anything in life apart from the threat to one of my children. I'm clinging to the hope that perhaps Carl's lying. That she's really with him and he's just trying to prove a point. That's definitely the better of the two evils.

Or maybe when I get back to the hotel she'll be there now, waiting for me. We'll have somehow missed each other as we left the Turkish Baths and we'll laugh about how daft we are and how much of a state I've got myself into.

But no, there's absolutely no sign of her. I check with the hotel manager for messages before ordering a large wine and sitting at a table by the pool, the call to prayer once again filling my ears. *I'm praying for Hayley,* I whisper into the darkness. *Please God, let her walk in here right now. Please, please let her be alright.*

Four glasses of wine and two hours later, she still isn't back. I've pressed redial on her phone more times than I could possibly count and another curt reply from Carl maintains he still hasn't heard from her either. I'm certain that by now he'd have admitted having her if that were the case.

And there's been nothing from the police yet. I *have* to trust that they're looking for her, as they promised. What if Jay's instructed someone to take her and she's being held somewhere? What if she's been hurt? Or worse?

I return to our room, curl up on my bed and howl like a wounded animal.

17

DEBRA

I WAKE with a start and tilt my watch to my face. As is the case every night when I wake, it's dead on 3am. I'm fully clothed, my head's pounding and my mouth feels like something's died in it. I sit up, expecting to see the outline of my daughter as she sleeps in the bed beside me. But then it hits me like a train.

She's missing. And I haven't seen her since just after six last night.

I snap the bedside lamp on and stumble to the bathroom for some water. Then I return to the room. What am I supposed to do now? I can't just lie here, waiting. And there's certainly no chance of any more sleep. The wine helped me to pass out before and I'm amazed really that I've managed to sleep for over three hours. I'm a despicable mother. I've slept whilst my daughter could be *anywhere*. And *anything* could be happening to her. I check my phone again. I try ringing her. This is an absolute nightmare and I can't bear it for much longer.

As I lean back on my pillows, I recall that this is how she and Lance will have spent the night when they were waiting for Bryn's body to be identified. The night when they couldn't get in touch with me. What I did to them was unforgivable and this could be my

98

punishment. What was it Dad always used to say to me? *What goes around comes around.*

It's the not knowing that's the worst thing. I close my eyes and try to talk to her in my head.

I'm so sorry sweetheart. Wherever you are, I'll find you. Please, please, please be safe.

If anything's happened to her, I'm going to go with her. I won't be able to go on.

As I sob into my pillow, trying to figure out whether I should return to that boat, the door bangs against the wall as it swings open.

'Mum!'

'Hayley! Thank God you're back. Where on earth have you been?'

She staggers in and sits on the edge of my bed. 'I thought that was *it* for me. I've never been so scared in all my life.'

I lunge towards her and throw my arms around her. 'Oh thank God you're safe,' I cry. 'I've been terrified.'

'They let me go. Oh, Mum, it was awful.'

'Who was it?' I pull her closer as she sobs into my shoulder. 'What have they done to you?' I can hardly bear to hear the answer. If they've violated her in any way, I'll be taking matters into my own hands.

'I was told to wait in this cubicle at the Turkish baths and then these men.' She gulps air in as she tries to get her words out.

'Take your time, sweetheart. It's OK. You're safe now.'

'I don't know who they were but they suddenly drew the curtain back and said I had to go with them. One of them had a knife.'

She's shaking uncontrollably in my arms. This is all my fault. I did this to her. Me, her mother, who's supposed to protect her, come what may.

'Did anyone hurt you.' I hold her away at arms length as I give her the once over.

'They threw me in the back of a van – that's where I've been – for hours and hours. I thought they were never going to let me go.'

I study her face, looking for signs she might have been hit, or worse. As if forcing her into a van at knifepoint isn't terrifying enough. But it could be worse. It could be so much worse.

'I have to ask.' I search for the right words. This is a question which no mother should ever have to ask. 'Did anyone—? did they try—?' I can't say the words. 'Hayley, no one tried to—?'

'No, Mum. That was the first thing that crossed my mind too. *What do they want with me? Are they going to rape me?*'

'Did the police find you? I reported you missing, of course I did. As soon as I realised you'd gone.'

'It was weird.' She's calming down a little now. 'After locking me in that van all night, suddenly, they just let me go. But I didn't have a clue where I was or how to get back here.' She wrings her hands in her lap. 'One of those yellow taxis stopped in the end – you know, like we got from the airport. I put my arm out and it stopped.'

I let a long breath out. Thank God she's alright. 'Have you been in touch with the police yet?'

'I just wanted to get back *here*. To *you*.' Her voice wobbles. 'I didn't even know *how* to call the police or what to say. They wouldn't have understood me anyway.'

'I should let them know you've come back. They're out there, looking. Where did they take you?'

'I don't know – I was just locked in the back of the van – there weren't any windows. Oh, Mum – I was in there for so long.' Fresh tears fill her eyes. 'They switched my phone off, and then took my bag away before slamming the door and locking me in. I had no idea what they were planning to do with me.'

'Oh, Hayley, I can't believe what you've been through.' I choke back tears. 'I'm just so sorry you had to go through this. If I could have gone in your place, of course I would.'

Her expression changes. 'Why would *you* be sorry? What could *you* have done to stop it from happening?' She fixes me with a curious stare.

'Didn't they say *anything* to you?'

Her face clouds over. 'Well, this is the thing. One of them spoke better English than the other and he said, 'Tell your mother this is a warning.'

Something in my belly gives way and for a moment, I think I might throw up. Jay's behind this – he has to be.

'What the hell was he on about, Mum?' Hayley's tone rises. 'Is this why you've just said you're sorry? What's going on?'

I'll have to tell her something of the truth – it's the only way I'm going to keep her safe until we get ourselves out of here. As if I was enjoying my own Turkish Bath experience while all the time some maniacs were bundling my girl into a van at knifepoint. Another nightmare I'll now have to live with.

'OK, I'm going to tell you what's been going on.' I take a deep breath and clasp my hands together as though praying she'll understand. 'Jay's here in Bodrum, love. Which is why I wanted to come here in the first place.'

She stares at me for a moment, the silence of the night hanging between us.

'What do you mean?' She swipes at her tears. 'I thought we were coming here for a holiday together. I thought you wanted to spend some time with *me*.'

'I did. I do – of course I do. But listen,' I reach for her and rest my hand on her arm. 'I'm going to tell you the truth.'

'It's about time by the sounds of it.'

'I should have told you sooner but you had more than enough to cope with losing your dad so horrifically.'

'Is there anything to drink in that fridge?' She rises from the bed. She's definitely her mother's daughter.

'Only water, I'm afraid, love. If there'd been any wine, I'd have downed it by now. I've never been so scared as I have been tonight.'

This is a crass thing to say after what *she's* had to go through in the last few hours. I shouldn't be making *any* of it about me.

The room lights up some more as she opens the fridge, takes out a bottle of water and guzzles it before slamming the door shut again. It's possibly hours since she had a drink.

'Didn't they even give you water?' A vision of my poor daughter, thirsty, terrified and all alone in the back of some dirty van fills my mind.

She shakes her head as she wipes her lips on the back of her hand – a habit I used to tell her off for when she was small.

'Look, Mum – I'm OK, right? Very shaken up, but they didn't actually hurt me. I've still got my phone and my purse and I was able to get away from them. So just tell me what you've got to tell me.'

'Right – firstly, like I just said, Jay's here.'

'I should have known *he'd* be at the bottom of things.' I hate the way she's looking at me now. And she's every right to. After all, she knows I was prepared to leave her and Lance behind. That I was planning to put myself first and go travelling with Jay. She's just about forgiven me for that and then *this* happens.

I steel myself for the half-story I'm going to tell her. Hopefully, it will be enough. 'OK, I went to see Jay yesterday morning and threatened him. But then he threatened me back – something about *knowing* people. I should have said something before. If it wasn't for me...' My words trail off. I've got to be careful here. I can't tell her *everything*, just a watered-down version.

'What are you talking about? You *threatened* him?'

'When Jay left England at the New Year, he didn't just *leave*.'

'Meaning?'

'He also stole all my money from me.' I watch for her reaction, now noticing her grubby clothes and her hair as she stands in front of the lamp – it's wet with tears and matted from being God knows where for so long. Somehow I'll have to get her through this and help her put it behind her. The poor love. As if she hasn't been through enough already.

'How much?'

'Every penny, just about. This is why I had to move in with you. There's nothing left.'

'And there was me thinking you'd moved in because you didn't want to be on your own.' Her voice is a cross between disappointment and sarcasm and I don't really blame her. I don't think before I speak sometimes.

'There *was* that and obviously, I wanted to be around for you as well – but he really did take *everything*. He completely emptied my business account *and* the office safe – I haven't even been able to pay the staff what I owed them.'

She shakes her head. 'No wonder Janice was off with me when I told her we were going away.'

'I feel wretched at owing my staff money but coming here was the best chance of getting some of my money back and being able to comfortably pay them all. As soon as I found out where he was, I couldn't just leave it.'

'So he's *here*?' She points at the floor. 'In Bodrum? How did you find out?'

'I found where he's been working, through Facebook, well through his *girlfriend* actually.' The word *girlfriend* sticks in my throat. If they were to ever get married, I'd be the maniac woman at the back of the church, shrieking the words to the song, *it should have been me.*

'Where's he working?'

'The Dolphini Village. Close to that beach bar we were at yesterday.'

'I could tell you were distracted.'

That's an understatement. 'And he's been living on a boat.'

'You've done your homework then – but *how* did you threaten him?' Her voice rises. This is it – this is where we start getting into the nitty-gritty of it all.

'I told him that unless he pays me fifty grand of my money back, I'm going to the police – now that I know where he is.'

'Why didn't you go to the police in the first place?' She's looking at me as if I'm deranged. Maybe I am. 'And why,' she continues, 'is this the first I'm hearing about any of this?'

She's far too grown up for her age, my daughter, and somehow always manages to make me feel as if I'm being chastised.

'I just felt such a fool, love. I fell for all Jay's crap, hook, line and sinker, didn't I?'

Jennefer's words resound in my head. *You're making a fool of yourself,* she told me. *He's only interested in your money.* As things have turned out, it's been an expensive lesson to learn.

'Besides, I had no idea where he'd gone,' I say. 'I only found out that day you saw me looking at flights and hotels.'

'Then why didn't you go to the police, *then?*' In the dim lamplight, Hayley's expression is somewhere between puzzled and angry. I deserve her anger after what she's been through over these last few endless hours.

'I don't really have a sensible answer. I guess it's because I'd have *no* chance of ever getting any of it back if I had. I'd have to *prove* he robbed me.'

'Why couldn't you?'

'Because I gave him access to the safe and the business account. They'd have said I deserved all I got.' I sigh. 'And I probably did.'

'So how did he threaten *you?*'

'He told me he *knew* people.' I hang my head. He certainly wasn't lying. 'But I honestly thought he was directing his threat at *me.* If I'd thought for one minute he'd come after you...'

'You need to keep away from him, Mum. You've got to let the police deal with him – I can't see any other way.'

'I know.'

But what I'm *not* going to tell her, is the other way I already have planned.

18

TINA

'Do you believe her when she says she hasn't got any money left?' I glance up from buttering my toast. '*You* know the woman better than I do. I only ever really spoke to her that time on the train.'

A vision of Debra sitting beside me on New Year's Day fills my mind. All perfume, poise and perfect nails. And while we rough it with jam on toast, she'll be sitting pretty with some waiter-served continental breakfast. She won't be watching every penny like Carl and I are having to do.

My son agreed to risk his freedom and even his *life* to carry out the dirty work associated with that fire and look where it's got him. Absolutely nowhere and he's been left with *nothing*.

'I don't know Debra all that well.' Carl turns from where he's been staring out of the window. 'To be honest, only Hayley's dad gave me the time of day and spoke to me like I was a fellow human instead of some kind of insect.'

'It makes me so angry to hear you say that.'

'It was obvious from the moment Debra clapped eyes on me, that she couldn't bear me around. Or to have Hayley anywhere near me.'

I shake my head. I know better than anyone what Carl's faults are, but he's such a good-looking lad and able to turn on the charm when it suits him, that it's hard to believe he couldn't have somehow won her over. From everything he's told me and from what Debra said to me on the train, it sounds like he never stood a chance. I only wish I'd known she was talking about *him*. She'll have her sights set on Hayley getting with some hotshot barrister with a fat wallet. That's what it always boils down to, especially where people like Debra are concerned. *How much money have you got?* Or in our case, *how much money haven't you got?*

'I'm sick of it.'

'What?'

I slide the butter back into the fridge. Just thirty minutes in the heat of this apartment would liquidise it. I'm surprised it hasn't liquidised *me* yet.

'People looking down their noses at us. Treating us like we're not good enough.'

'To answer your earlier question, I reckon she'd have agreed to pay us off if she had the money.' Carl sits on the window sill, the bus station behind him in full swing. As if we've got *that* for a view from our window.

'Really?' Surely he isn't sticking up for her now.

'Debra wouldn't risk us telling Hayley — or anyone else. From what I know, her main focus is what other people think about her. She wouldn't want what she's done to get out.'

'You've mellowed since we set off.' I narrow my eyes at him. He really has. There was far more anger in him when we were back in Yorkshire. 'You seem to be going soft all of a sudden. What's got into you?'

He stands from the windowsill and shuffles from foot to foot.

'Come on – out with it.'

'If you must know, me and Hayley have been messaging for the last couple of days.' He avoids my gaze but can't disguise the smirk that crosses his face as he looks at his feet. He seems happy about this latest development.

I however, am not. I nearly spit my toast out. He's such a dark horse. 'You've been *messaging* each other? About *what*?'

Talk about muddying the waters – especially if he means what I think he means.

'This and that. Come on, Mum. Do I quiz you about people you might be messaging with?'

'I think this is different, don't you?' I lean against the kitchen counter as I continue to watch him. 'Does *Hayley* know we're here?'

'Not yet.' He runs his fingers through his fringe. He looks so much like his father used to – the man I hardly know anymore. I wish he'd just leave with the woman he's been seeing. But he won't. He's made it perfectly clear he wants *me* to leave. But he'll set up house with her in my home over my dead body.

'And maybe I'll keep it that way,' Carl goes on. 'Depending on what happens.'

'What do you mean?'

'If she finds out we're over here and so close to her and her mother – well, I don't want to creep her out, do I?'

'I take it there's a chance of you getting back together?' Bloody hell, after everything that's gone on, I can't believe this.

'I don't know. She's being friendlier than she has for months so I'm just going with the flow.'

'Well this complicates things, don't you think? How can we go in all heavy-handed if you and her are—'

'Which is why I've decided to go to Jay directly for our money,' he tells me.

'I don't like the sound of this.' I tip my other slice of toast into the bin. Suddenly I'm not hungry.

'We've found where he's staying, haven't we? *And* where he's working. So I was thinking I might pay him a little visit.'

'When?

'Sooner rather than later.'

'And then what?'

'I really don't think he's got a clue that I saw him running away after starting the fire. So now I know where to find him, I can make him aware of what I've got.'

'Seeing him's one thing – proving it will be quite another.'

'A time and date stamped photo should be enough of a convincer for him to see things our way.'

'You *never* told me about that.' As I stare at him in amazement, something lifts within me. We're getting nowhere with Debra, but Carl having this photo could change *everything*.

'I haven't *really* got a photo.' Carl must notice how far my expression falls as he quickly says, 'But Jay doesn't need to know that, does he? Also, when I fill him in about everything Debra divulged to *you* on that train journey – that she was planning to set Bryn up all along...'

'Hmm, I guess, it *could* still all go in our favour. It better had, otherwise we've come all this way for nothing.' I sigh again, more deeply this time.

'It's got to be worth a try?' He continues. 'I'm going to get him on his own and tell him we want twenty grand not to report him and Debra.'

'Make it thirty,' I tell him. 'I've got to pay the money back into your grandma's account yet, haven't I? So when are you going to see him?' I don't even know that I should be encouraging this but it certainly sounds more hopeful than trying to squeeze blood from the stone that is Debra.

Carl taps his watch. 'Well, there's no time like the present – the early bird and all that.'

'There *is* another option here, you know.' It suddenly occurs to me.

'What?'

'Rather than *threatening* him that you'll go to the police, you could offer to join forces with him against Debra. That might be worth something.'

'I don't see what good that would do,' he replies. 'If Debra's telling the truth and if she really *doesn't* have any money, it won't matter who joins forces with who.'

19

DEBRA

IT'S NO GOOD. I can't lie here a moment longer. I need to move – I need to get out of this room.

It was nearly daylight by the time Hayley settled down enough to be able to sleep after her ordeal. Since she went off, she's barely moved and I've watched her as closely as I did when she was a newborn. The blackout curtains and the white noise from the air conditioning unit should ensure she stays this way for a few hours longer at the very least.

I throw back my sheet and lay my bare feet on the floor. This insomnia is crucifying me – I don't know how much longer I can stand it. I've even Googled to find out how little sleep a person can survive on before insomnia kills them – I've tried all the hints and tips to sleep but nothing seems to work. Perhaps nothing ever will.

One of the suggestions, however, is no matter how exhausted you're feeling, to make sure to get some exercise. It's still early so the pool should be empty. I part the curtains and glance out. Alas, there are four young kids and a dad in there, having a whale of a time with their inflatables and a snorkel. The mother of the family has no doubt kicked them all out of their apartment so *she* can have some peace.

I need to clear my mind – I need to think. The beach would be better than this place and at this hour, there should hardly be anyone around.

So slipping my cossie on and then my dress over the top of it, I grab a towel and my phone before sliding my feet into flip-flops.

Hayley hasn't moved. If she wakes to find I'm not here, she'll be really upset – especially after last night. I'd better leave her a note.

I needed to get out love, so am just going down to the beach for a quick swim. I'm locking you in with my key but I should be back before you wake up. I've got my phone on me if you wake up first. Hope you're feeling better this morning - love you zillions!
xx

Tears fill my eyes. When she was a little girl it was our game after I'd tucked her in at night. *Love you hundreds* became, thousands, millions, billions, trillions and zillions. I've really, really let her down – Lance too. A swim will help me think straight and work out a way forward from all this, especially after what happened last night, even if that's just cutting our losses and returning to Yorkshire. To be honest, that's starting to sound more appealing than anything.

I leave the note with her key on top of the kettle. I imagine that will be one of the first places she goes if she does happen to wake before I get back.

～

As expected at this hour, there isn't a soul around on this side of the bay. It's a spot our hotelier recommended when we arrived. This is what I need, solitude, sunshine and the open water all to myself.

I kick off my sandals, slot my phone inside one of them, my hotel key in the other and then leave them behind a rock with my dress and towel laid over the top. I gingerly walk over the pebbles, feeling the pain of each one underfoot. If I could swap the heat and blue waves for the sand of a Yorkshire beach, it would be the perfect combination.

The cool water is a shock to the system at first but I quickly get used to it as I kick my legs and venture away from the shore. This is what it feels like to be alive. All I've been doing lately is existing rather than living.

As I head out into the waves, rather than mulling over each and every possibility of what I could do to fix things, my head instead begins to clear and I have a sense of freedom unlike anything I've felt for a while. It's as if I've left all my problems piled up with my belongings. Out here I'm at one with nature – free and invincible – somewhere no one can reach me.

It's a joy to break free of the dragging thoughts of all that's going on. To just be *me* for half an hour. This is what I need – *me time*. This was part of the reason I was running away with Jay in the first place. I'd been swallowed whole by my existence as wife, mother and pub owner, and then when the kids moved out, a part of me went with them, and suddenly, I didn't even know who I was anymore. All that mixed in with my hormones, not to mention my achingly boring marriage, it was little wonder I inflicted the damage I've managed to do to myself.

The ocean's so blue, it's impossible to discern where the horizon meets the sky. The sun's risen high enough to cast its rays as diamonds dancing on each ripple. I'm going to make the most of every second out here. As soon as I return to the shore, the problems will all be still there stacked up beside my clothes. My guilt, my blackmailers, the threat to my daughter and the fact that I've been fleeced out of everything I ever worked for. They'll all be waiting for me.

It sounds like wind at first but before long, I realise the humming is an approaching speedboat. That's all I need – whenever I'm doing something I enjoy, something always happens to spoil it. I just hope whoever's on it doesn't decide to dock here. Knowing my luck, they'll try to make conversation with me. When the last thing I can be bothered with is small talk.

The hum's becoming more of a roar. Its driver could have chosen *any* bit of this shoreline but no, they have to come in *my* direction. I pause to tread water while cursing the fact that the calm and smooth surface is already beginning to churn up with the motion of the speedboat's approach. With the current now against me, to get anywhere is like trying to swim through treacle.

Then a dreadful thought washes over me – has the driver of the speedboat even *seen* me?

I tread water while waving my arms in the air – the sun's behind the speedboat – in my eyes, rather than in theirs. It's close enough now to easily spot me as I bob around on the surface of the water.

But bloody hell, it still seems to be heading *straight* in my direction. I glance back to the shore, the rock where I've left my belongings looking like a long way away. With the breeze behind me, I didn't realise I'd swum this far out.

The speedboat is closing the gap between us, the engine growing louder. I need to get out of its way, and quickly. The driver doesn't seem to have seen me.

Only they must have done. And as I attempt to swim to the left, the driver's direction adjusts as well. Oh my God, oh my God, I'm going to be lucky if it misses me here.

There's a split second in which the driver and I lock eyes while I make one last move to get out of the way. But the engine noise vibrates through me and a searing pain shoots through my shoulder. Suddenly, I'm on my back, my eyes wide open. Somehow I'm still floating on the surface. I'm still here. I'm still alive.

I spit the salty water, or could it be blood, from my mouth. As I squint at the rear of the speedboat, I realise I've got a chance to get away. But it's turning around. As it spins in the waves, I gasp. It's heading back at me.

And this time it's right on target.

PART II

HAYLEY

20

HAYLEY

FOR A FEW MOMENTS, I wonder where I am when I wake. Then as I glance around at the brightly-coloured decor and the paintings of the Bodrum view from the shore and harbour, I remember – I'm away with Mum. Supposedly, on holiday. One of the pictures shows the view she and I looked over as we dined on our first night here. She seemed more on edge than I'd ever seen her that evening. And now I know why.

I used to tease Mum about flirting with Jay when she first took him on at the pub. She began taking more pride in her appearance than ever before and acting like a lovesick teenager whenever he was around. Lance and I might have joked she was having a mid-life crisis but I was more worried about her making a fool of herself than anything else. Dad, on the other hand, told me he'd had an awful feeling about Jay from the moment he set eyes on him. I tried to reassure him but it turned out he was right.

I've got a splitting headache after last night. It'll be partly down to how terrified I was, coupled with the dehydration after being abandoned for so long without water. Somehow, the lowlifes who imprisoned me in the back of that van will get what's coming to them. I don't know how, but I'll find a way.

'Mum,' I call. It's another beautiful day, judging by the sunshine that's bleeding around the edges of the curtains. She must be in the loo or getting dried from the shower. She'll have some headache tablets in her bag – she's always like a walking pharmacy.

She doesn't answer. I bet she's out there, sunning herself. My head swoons as I get to my feet and lurch towards the balcony doors. As I reach them, I check my watch. Bloody hell – it's nearly noon. I can hardly believe I've wasted an entire morning when I could have been out there, allowing the sun to help me feel better. I've even missed breakfast, which stopped being served an hour ago. The rumble in my belly reminds me of the fact that I haven't eaten a thing since our lunch in the beach bar yesterday. I pull the curtains back and allow my gaze to roam around the perimeter of the pool. But there's no sign of Mum and suddenly I have echoes of when she disappeared with her anxiety attack the other evening.

Hmm. After what happened to me last night, she *surely* can't have gone far. Perhaps she's in the shade of the bar area with a book and a coffee. Any other possibilities don't bear thinking about. For instance, if she's gone after Jay again. It really sounds like *he* was behind me being bundled into that van.

Perhaps she's with the police – yes, that's the most likely scenario although I still can't believe she's just buggered off while I'm sleeping.

I reach for my phone in case she's tried ringing or sending a text but the only message is from Carl – a couple of hours ago.

> Morning H. Hope you're having a good time. I'm glad we're messaging and hope you meant what you said about meeting up sometime. Hope it wasn't the wine talking. Cxx

Mum would have a fit if she knew Carl and I were texting again. He's started just using our initials in his messages, like we used to when we were together. He sent his first text on the day of Dad's funeral, saying he hoped I hadn't minded him paying his respects.

He added that he'd wanted to come over and ask how I was coping but hadn't liked to intrude, especially after how he and I had fallen out so spectacularly.

I was feeling so low that day that I ended up replying and it's just gone from there. We haven't met up or anything yet but I'm beginning to seriously consider it. After all, his messages remind me of how he was in the beginning. Maybe he's changed. Perhaps he's learned from everything that went wrong between us. People do change. Don't they?

I cast my gaze around the pool again. *Where the hell is my mother?*

Glancing back into the room, I can see that her bag's still here which is reassuring as she doesn't usually go too far without it. Then I spot a torn-off piece of paper on top of the kettle and anxiety begins to flutter in my belly.

The fact she's suggesting she'll be back before I wake means she'll have gone fairly early for her swim. So surely she'd be back by now? I reach again for my phone and try her number. It just rings out before eventually reaching voicemail.

'Mum, it's me. I don't know where you are but please just let me know you're OK. Honestly, we need to start tracking each other.' I laugh as I press the end-call button.

Tracking each other wouldn't be such a bad idea. Particularly while we're here, in this strange country where seemingly, anything could happen.

As I wait for the kettle to boil, I've got an awful feeling in the pit of my stomach and it isn't just due to not eating last night or this morning. Something feels wrong.

The sun lounger I've settled on might be in the shade but it has the best view of the entrance gate. When that errant mother of mine returns, I'm going to go crazy with her. She *promised* me she wouldn't involve herself directly with Jay any further. She'll have to cut her losses and chalk up the money she lost to experience. I know from the altercation I had with him on New Year's Day how pig-headed and narcissistic he is.

If she lied to me about keeping away – if really, she's gone off to confront him over what happened to me, who knows how he could react? If she'd just gone to the police to report it, surely they'd have wanted to speak to *me* by now to corroborate whatever she's told them. I've been awake for well over an hour – time enough for them to turn up here with Mum if that *is* where she went.

'You order lunch?' A staff member places a menu on the table beside me.

'Erm yes, I will, thanks.'

'I come back,' she announces as I begin to study it.

The stress of not knowing where Mum is has killed my hunger but I know I've got to eat something or I'll keel over in this heat.

By the time my sandwich and wine arrive, I've left Mum another voicemail, sent another text and looked to see when she was last active on both Whatsapp and Messenger. Not since late last night, which isn't like her at all. She's never off Facebook, normally. Another thing Lance and I used to poke fun at her about.

I can't imagine her doing something like going shopping after her swim. But if swimming was all she was doing, she should have been back *ages* ago. I'll finish my food, and then I'll go looking for her. I bet she's gone to the place that was suggested we swim at when we first arrived.

It's a fifteen-minute walk, according to Christina who manages the hotel. I don't think for one minute that Mum will still be there when I arrive but I can't just sit around here doing nothing. After what happened to *me* last night, I need to know she's safe.

As I reach the end of the lane, I turn towards the beach and unscrew the lid from my water bottle. I've only been walking for ten minutes and the water's already warm. The blue of the ocean is in sight now, so within a few minutes, I'll at least be able to rule this place out. But I haven't a clue where to look for her next if she isn't here. I could wander around the bars and shops but it would be like looking for a needle in a haystack. I daren't go to the police just yet and in any case, I wouldn't be able to make myself understood if I did.

The bay's packed with sunbathers. I scan from left to right and back again. When Christina recommended it, she mentioned that early mornings and evenings are the best times to swim. Any other times of day are usually heaving, she said. She wasn't wrong. The entire area's awash with colour and buzzing with enjoyment.

I head further onto the beach – I must be the only person here who's alone. It would be helpful if I'd known what colour clothing Mum's wearing – she might be easier to spot amongst this throng of people. I sigh. It's no good – I'll have to comb the entire area to check if she's here or not.

I head down to the water's edge and glance to the left where a flash of green is visible behind a rock. That looks like the colour of one of Mum's cardigans – one which I know for a fact that she's brought to Turkey. It looks like I've managed to find her straight away.

I scan the water but there's no sign of her head bobbing above the waves. I run over to the rock, hoping it really *is* her stuff and that I'm not suddenly going to be accosted by someone who thinks I'm trying to rob them. It's Mum's stuff alright. Her dress, cardigan, sandals, phone and hotel keycard.

I just need to find *her* now.

21

HAYLEY

AT LEAST SHE can't be far.

I pick up her phone, and see several missed calls on her lock screen and the start of a message from... *Carl*!

Why would *he* be messaging Mum? I don't understand.

Since you haven't contacted me or answered my mum's messages, I'm—

What the hell's all that about? *My mum's messages?* What's his mum got to do with *mine*? And why would Carl be messaging my mum anyway? That's if this is even the same Carl. For all I know, Mum could have met someone else. I can't imagine she'd have the energy – since the New Year, she's looked like she has the weight of the world on her shoulders.

I scan the water again, looking for her blonde head. She normally has it scraped into a bun when she's swimming. I scan further out – but she can't be too far away – not when she's left her phone here. She wouldn't have let it out of her sight for too long.

I head to the water's edge, the joviality of those enjoying themselves shredding every one of the nerves I have left. The shrieks of carefree laughter couldn't be any more at odds with the angst that's swirling around inside me. Normally I'd paddle amongst them and enjoy the sight of the sunlight dancing on the waves but instead, the dread within my belly is intensifying. I can't see her. Oh my God, I really can't see her.

I have a feeling just like I had on the first of January when I knew something had happened – I just didn't know the *what* or the *who*.

Mum – where the bloody hell are you? I tug my phone from my bag and try ringing Carl through Messenger. He doesn't answer so I fire a message off.

> Carl, I could really do with speaking to you as soon as possible.

Normally, I'd put a smiley face on my messages to him. Not a kiss though – not since we parted company last November. I'm not sure if I want to get back with him, not after the way he treated me before we split and then the way he stalked me after that was pretty unnerving. I shiver, which in the heat of the day is also unnerving. Something's wrong here – really wrong.

I glance up from my screen, letting my gaze roam back over the bay and around the groups of people in clusters across the beach. Perhaps Mum's got talking to someone. After so many years of being a gregarious pub landlady, she loves being around people and has always had the gift of the gab. It was something Dad hated about her but only, as she's so often pointed out, because he was so insecure.

My chest tightens as once again, I fail to find her. I check my phone – there's nothing back from Carl yet. I can't do this on my own so I pull Lance's number up and hit call. Mum will string me up for worrying him but he'd do the same if he were in my shoes.

He answers on the third ring. 'To what do I owe this pleasure, sis?'

'I can't find Mum.' I can't keep the panic from my voice as I blurt the situation to him.

'You're in Turkey! What on earth do you want me to do from Leicester.' He laughs.

'I know it sounds daft but I'm really worried. I've just found her clothes, shoes and phone next to a rock in a bay but there's no sign of her anywhere.'

'When did you last see her?' His tone flattens out and I feel wretched for dragging him into it.

'It was the middle of the night actually.' I won't tell him yet about my ordeal – there'll be time for all that later. Right now the only thing that matters is finding Mum. 'She left a note this morning, saying she was going for a swim when I was still asleep. I'm not sure what time but it could have been hours ago.'

He falls silent for a moment. 'I'm sure she won't be far, Hayles. Honestly, you're probably just overreacting after all we've been through with Dad.'

'It's just really odd. Have *you* heard anything from her this morning?'

'Nope. I haven't heard from her for a day or two, nor did I expect to. You're both on holiday, aren't you?' There's an edge to his words, making me feel even guiltier. Obviously he should be here with us. And I wish he was.

'Do you know anything about her messaging with Carl?'

'Carl?' He sounds shocked. 'As in your *ex*, Carl?'

'I think so. As far as I know, she doesn't know any other Carls. There's a message on her lock screen from him – I don't know what to think if I'm honest.' *Mum and Carl*, no, surely not.

'The only reason she'd be messaging with *him* would be to warn him off you.' I imagine Lance frowning as he says this. He's never been able to stand my ex.

'That's what I'd have said.' It's good to hear him affirm what I'm already thinking.

'Have you and him been back in touch or something?' His tone becomes accusatory. If I do get back with Carl, after everything I've said about him, things will be far from plain sailing where my family and friends are concerned.

'Nope.' It's a blatant lie, of course it is, but until I've decided what the way forward might be on that score, I'm not saying anything to anyone, not even my brother, who I usually trust with most things. 'I'm starting to wonder if I should report her missing.'

'Are there any islands she might have swum to? Or boats?'

I glance across the sparkling blue water – it looks inviting and I'm so hot, I'd love to peel my clothes off and dive right in. But until I lay eyes on my mother, I can't do anything else other than to keep looking. 'Nothing I can see,' I reply. 'It's a complete mystery.'

'Is there a coastguard around? Like we have over here? If you're really worried, you should report it. What if she's been swept away?'

'It's not that kind of sea here. Honestly, the weather couldn't be any nicer today – it's barely blowing a breeze.' Of course, I can't tell him what I'm really worried about. Of Jay's potential involvement in all this. Lance doesn't need to know about any of that just yet. There'll be time later if it comes to it. I've still got to get my own head around things.

'You'll find her – I know you will.'

'I'll have another wander round and if I don't find her in the next five minutes, I'll go across to the coastguard and get some help.'

'I'd go to them sooner rather than later, Hayles. If she *is* in any trouble out there...' His voice trails off. The two of us have already had to grow up by ten years in four months to cope with what happened. I don't think we could cope with any more.

'I've got savings in my account if you want me to come out, sis.'

'I don't think there's any need for that just yet. I rang you mainly to check if you'd heard from her.'

'If I do, I'll call you straight away.'

'Well, her phone's here, like I said,' – I glance towards the rock – 'so unless she calls you from someone else's.'

'Just keep me posted, Hayles. Honestly, I can't believe we're having to worry about Mum again. I wonder who's the parent out of us all at times.'

I laugh though it sounds hollow. 'I know exactly what you mean.'

I feel slightly better for hearing my brother's voice – more grounded somehow. I picture him in my head. Six foot three with his size eleven feet – but still with the baby face I always loved to squeeze. And I'm so glad Sophie came straight back to him when she heard the news about Dad. I've never challenged her about their split – I just hope she's back for keeps. It seems I have enough with keeping my eye on Mum, without having to worry about Lance as well.

As soon as I've ended the call with my brother, I try Carl on Messenger again and sink to sit on the pebbles. For a time after our relationship ended, I deleted his number and blocked him on Facebook. Therefore it feels strange to have unblocked him and to have his name showing in my Messenger contacts again. Still, there's no reply. It's one thirty in the afternoon here so ten thirty in the UK. He'll be working – but I can't imagine he's too far away from his phone – he never is. But none of this solves the mystery of where the hell my mother is.

And I can't shake the fear that she's been grabbed and thrown into the back of a van like I was last night.

Or worse.

22

HAYLEY

'DO YOU SPEAK ENGLISH?' I run up to a couple nearest the rock where my mother's belongings are. The man shrugs his shoulders and the woman shakes her head, an apologetic expression on her face.

I run to a family a few metres from them. 'Do you speak English?' With their pale, freckly skin, they *look* English and possibly like they've recently arrived.

'Yes,' the woman replies. 'Are you OK?' I want to hug her in relief. Maybe she's seen Mum.

I point at the rock. 'My mum's left her things there and I think she's gone for a swim. But there's no sign of her and as far as I know, she could have gone in the water a while ago.' I'm gabbling away here, probably making little sense as my words tumble over each other. 'It could have been as early as first thing this morning when she went in there.' I gesture across the water and tears fill my eyes as the magnitude of what I'm saying hits me. It's starting to feel real. 'She should have been back ages ago.'

'What does your mum look like?' The man follows my gaze out to sea.

'She's fifty, about five foot six, she's got blonde hair, she usually has it tied up, she's slim...' My voice trails off.

'If you're worried, you should definitely report her missing,' the woman says. 'We haven't seen anyone near that rock since we got here – and that' – she glances at her watch – 'was nearly two hours ago.'

'Did you notice her things there when you arrived?'

She shakes her head. 'We've had our attention on the kids to be honest.' She nods to a group of kids at the water's edge. 'I'm really sorry I can't be any more help. Do you want me to come with you to find the coastguard?'

'It's fine.' I force a smile. 'I don't want to interrupt your day any more than I already have. Thanks for listening.'

'Keep us posted,' she says, echoing Lance's words. 'We'll be here for a while yet. If there's anything we can do...'

'Thank you.' I step away from them, casting my eyes for what feels like the hundredth time across the bay, willing, with every fibre of my being, for my mother to materialise. Perhaps I should have accepted that woman's offer to come with me. I'm suddenly reminded of Alan, the wonderful taxi driver who didn't leave my side in the aftermath of the fire. Without him, I'd have fallen apart even more than I did while I was waiting for Lance to be driven back from university.

It's no good. I'll have to report her missing – I don't know what else to do.

Finally, having eventually made myself understood with the help of Google translate and the coastguard's broken English, a boat is going out to look for her. All I can do is wait.

He's given me a bottle of water and as I sit on the pebbles, with my knees hugged into my chest, I feel well and truly numb. Exactly like I did when that body was lying in the tent in the pub's car park.

I watch on as helplessly as I did then with no one telling me a thing. I don't know what's worse, the not knowing or the closure that comes with the answers when all hope has been snatched away. I could tell from the coastguard's face that my mother's possessions being disregarded for so long, coupled with her note suggesting she left early morning were causes enough for concern.

I can't get to my phone fast enough as it rings inside my bag.

'Have you found her yet?' Lance's voice is full of hope and expectation.

I'd give anything to be able to say yes and put my brother's mind at rest. 'Oh Lance, I'm terrified.' I can't keep the wobble from my voice. 'I've reported her missing.'

'So what's happening?' He sounds so far away. It's not like New Year's Day when he was just a motorway drive's distance from me.

'The coastguards are about to go looking. They've cleared everyone from the water and are launching the boat now.' I watch them scramble into it while several disgruntled swimmers throw their arms in the air – no doubt because their swim has been cut short. I fight the urge to march over and demand to know how they'd feel if *their* mother had gone missing.

'Oh sis, I don't like the sound of this. Are you there on your own?'

I need Lance at my side more than ever. I can't believe this is happening. Not after what I went through last night. Mum's disappearance must have something to do with Jay – there's no other explanation.

'Hayley?'

'Yes. I'm on my own. And I don't know what to do. I've never felt so useless.' That's a lie – of course I have. And not that long ago.

'They'll find her Hayles. Just sit tight.'

'That's almost what I'm scared of. What if something—' My voice trails off. I can't say what I'm thinking out loud. Mum can swim but she's not the strongest swimmer in the world. We used to laugh at her for just bobbing up and down at the local baths.

Pootling, she called it. She certainly wouldn't have won any medals for technique or speed but she said it cleared her head. But this isn't a swimming pool. There'll be undercurrents out there which might have pulled her down or she could have had some sort of medical emergency without anybody seeing her. My mind's spinning so fast, it's making me dizzy.

'She'll be fine, you'll see. There'll be a logical explanation. Listen, sis—'

'What?' Suddenly, he's acting like *he's* the older sibling and trying to reassure me.

'I'm going to get off this phone and start looking at flights. You know, just in case.'

'I don't think there's any need for that yet. Let's just sit tight like you said – I'll keep you posted.'

'As *soon* as you know anything. I'll just be here, in my room. I can't go into my last lecture with this buzzing around my head – not until they've found Mum.'

'I'm sorry I've dragged you into all this, bro.' Tears fill my eyes. The boat has disappeared around the corner of the bay and is heading further out. *Please, Mum – please be alright.*

'I'd have killed you if you hadn't let me know, Hayles. You can't go through all this on your own.'

Since everyone's been asked to leave the water, the bay's emptied considerably to what it was when I arrived. And without the sea to cool off in, it's no wonder. Those that remain are rubberneckers who'll have heard on the grapevine that a woman's gone missing. No doubt our plight will be posted all over social media before long – with everyone an amateur sleuth, all with their own theories of what might have happened.

Every time I glance around, people are pointing and looking at me, but instead of pointing their cameras at the search operation or me as I'd feared they might, most of their faces bear similar expressions of sympathy to those around me on New Year's Day. The family with the woman who offered to accompany me left ten minutes ago, but she gave me her number in case I need anything.

Yes, my mother to turn up safely.

I haven't had the chance to tell anyone yet about the potential connection to what's going on here with Jay – with a bit of luck, Mum will turn up before that becomes necessary. What an absolute nightmare.

After what feels like an eternity, there's a sudden flurry of activity behind me. My stomach lurches as several emergency vehicles screech into the entrance to the bay. Police officials jump from them and set about clearing the last of the people who remain here. The heavy hand of one of them rests on my shoulder and words are spoken to me in Turkish.

'She's my mother.' I can barely get my words out as I point out to sea. 'You can't make me leave.'

'Are you English?' He frowns but his hand doesn't leave me.

I nod. 'What's going on? Please tell me. Have they found something?' There has to be a reason why all these emergency workers have just arrived.

'Wait here.' He strides away, says something to his colleague and they both hurry back towards me. I can hardly breathe as one of them opens his mouth to speak.

'Are you her daughter?' The second man asks me. 'Debra Ford?'

'Yes. Please tell me what's happening.'

'They've found a woman.' He gestures to our right. 'On the rocks.'

My head swims and I'm suddenly back in my lounge standing beside Lance as the police faced us to break the inevitable news about Dad. We knew what they were about to say as soon as we saw their faces. It's about to happen all over again with Mum. I can't take it – I just can't take it. We can't lose both our parents in the space of a few months. It's a good thing I'm sitting down as I feel faint.

'Is she—' I can't say the word. Her face emerges in my mind. She has her faults, of course she has, but she's my absolute best friend. 'Please tell me she's not—' My words are swallowed by a helicopter and I notice some medics, or at least that's what I think they are, as they rush past me with a spinal board. These observations are hopeful. They must mean she's still alive.

'She told us her name—'

'So she's OK?'

'I'm sorry. She woke up just for a moment. She's being taken in air ambulance,' the officer tells me. 'We will take you to hospital in the car.'

'What's happened?' I close my eyes for a moment. 'Will she be alright?'

He gestures to his radio. 'She is not good. Loss of blood and snapped bone. They do their best to help. Let's get you to the car.'

'I'll get her things.' I point at the rock where they are. Other than her phone and the hotel key which is in my pocket. The bay swoons as I get to my feet and the officer catches me as I sway.

'Are you OK?'

'I'm just hot and I'm really scared.'

'We go to the car.' Not letting go of my arm, he steers me in the opposite direction to the rock. 'We need her things,' he seems to search for the right word. 'As evidence,' he affirms.

I'm handed another bottle of water as we reach the car and the air conditioning which washes over me is a blessed relief as I settle into the seat and close my eyes. *What am I like?* My mother's critically injured and I'm worrying about how hot I feel.

'Is she still lying there?' I point back towards the rocks where she's been found. There's no sign of the helicopter taking off yet.

'They take good care with her.' His expression is grave as he twists in his seat to look at me. 'They will look after her. We will look after you.'

'I need to ring my brother,' I say, hitting Lance's number on my phone. He answers before the first ring which is a first for him. Normally it goes to his voicemail.

'What's happening,' he demands. 'I'm going out of my mind here.'

'Oh, Lance.'

'What is it?' There's terror in his voice. 'Just tell me – *please!*'

'They've found Mum on some rocks – badly injured. She's being airlifted to hospital.'

'Oh my God – how badly injured?'

'I don't know – that's all they'll tell me.'

'Is she going to be OK?'

'I wish I knew.'

'You know Mum, she's made of steel.' He speaks with a conviction I wish I could rely on.

'I really hope so.'

'I'm going to book that flight.' His voice is filled with anguish. 'Where are they taking her?'

'I don't know yet. Just set off for Bodrum and there'll be a text waiting for you when you land to tell you where to go.'

Despite the horror of this, I'm strangely calmer than I was four months ago. Mum once said to me, *you'll never be given more hurt than you can handle.*

23

HAYLEY

She's in a bad way, bro but she's reasonably stable. She's out of it with all the painkillers. We're at the American hospital in Bodrum. I've been told it'll cost you about a thousand lira in a taxi which is about twenty-five quid, but they'll take pounds or euros if you didn't get any lira. We're still in the Emergency Room until they get a bed sorted for her. If she gets moved, I'll let you know. x

I'M TRACKING Lance's flight and he's about halfway here. I picture him, all alone on the plane and can't wait for him to arrive.

I stare down at Mum as the machines she's hooked up to bleep all around. The doctor had decent English and is reasonably hopeful she could be alright, subject to the brain scan she's in the queue for. Then they're deciding where to move her to. I'm praying she doesn't need intensive care as apparently, there aren't any beds today.

'I'm here, Mum.' I reach for her hand and tuck it into hers like I did when I was a little girl. 'Give me a squeeze if you can hear me.' The heat of tears returns to my eyes when she doesn't respond. I stare at the machine monitoring her heart rate, praying it keeps doing what it's doing. She's covered in some awful cuts and bruises and still needs stitches in a few of them. The x-ray has shown a broken collarbone, ankle, shoulder blade and wrist. As long as she gets through this, she's likely to be in hospital for a while.

'Sign here, ma'am.' I jump at the sudden voice behind me and let go of Mum's hand.

I take the clipboard from the nurse and look down at the form which is all in Turkish.

'Insurance.' She gestures to Mum. Thank God I ticked the box for holiday insurance. Dad would be proud of me for being responsible instead of trying to save a few quid like Lance would have done. My insides twist at the thought of my father. I sign my name and pass the clipboard back.

I reach for Mum's hand again. It's warm in mine as I stroke the top of it like she used to do with me as a child when I was ill. 'I'm not going anywhere.' I don't know if she can hear me, but I want her to know she's not on her own.

'Hayley Ford?' Another voice cuts through me. I've never felt as jumpy as I do right now. 'Is now a good time to answer some questions?' I twist in my seat to see a greying, thin woman accompanied by a burly police officer. 'I'm Cali Dobbs, and I'm going to act as your interpreter.' She gestures at the officer. 'Law Enforcement Officer Akbas and I won't keep you from your mother for long. The hospital staff have said we can use the room opposite to speak.'

As I get to my feet, I don't take my eyes away from Mum. I don't want to leave her alone for a second but the time has come to tell them what happened to me last night and how I believe it could be linked to what's happened today. It's also time to tell them about Mum coming here to go after Jay.

∾

'But you don't know *which* boat he's living on?' After I've regaled everything, the officer says something in Turkish, followed by the interpretor's question. 'Or where?'

I shake my head. 'I've no idea. Possibly on the harbour.' This won't be much help. It looks like there are at least a couple of hundred boats moored up there. 'But she's told me he works at a beach bar – but I'm sorry I can't bring the name to mind.'

She repeats what I've said and the officer writes something down.

I shuffle on the grey plastic sofa and glance at the door. I just want to get back to Mum and these people can then get out there looking for Jay.

The walls are closing in around me as I face my questioners. The room is sparse apart from the small plant and the box of tissues that sit on the dividing table. This room is clearly meant for agonising waits. A room where the worst news is imparted.

The interpretor says something to the officer who shakes his head before replying. This doesn't look great at all. Then she speaks again.

'What about last night, Hayley? Did you get a good look at the two men *or* the van you were driven away in?'

I shake my head. How can I tell her that most of the men I've seen in the bars and shops here all look so similar to me? Dark-haired, dark-skinned and stocky. Plus all I saw was the *inside* of the van. It was pitch black when they dumped me at the side of the road and I was disorientated. By the time I thought of getting its registration, it had sped away. 'Will there be cameras at the Turkish Baths?'

As she talks back to the officer, the other sounds of the unit swim around us. A child crying, the clanging of a trolley and the wail of a siren. I hate hospitals; it smells even more antiseptic in this one than it does in England, plus the stark, white walls with fluorescent light bouncing off them are making my headache even worse than it already was. The woman turns back to me. 'There could be cameras there, though it's unlikely – however, Officer Akbas says that will be one of the first lines of enquiry.'

The officer says something again, speaking at length for a few moments before the woman turns her attention to me.

'Do you have a photograph of this Jay Manningham?'

I shake my head. 'I don't know if there could still be one on my mother's phone. All her stuff has been taken for evidence. That's the only place I can think you'd find one. Or maybe there's one on line somewhere.'

'OK. There'll be something going out on the local news shortly. And clearly, we're all hoping for your mother to wake soon and be able to tell us exactly where we can find this man.'

'Can I get back to her now?'

'Of course, but if you think of *anything* that might help us, you should call this number straightaway.' She hands me a card.

At least they're looking for him. With information which points roughly to where he's living and working, it shouldn't be long before he's taken in.

I make my way back to where the police summoned me from. My focus has to be on Mum, it's *their* job to find Jay and I'm certain there'll be some camera footage *somewhere* to incriminate him. I draw back the curtain into the bay where Mum's been waiting for whatever comes next.

My heart literally stops as I stare at the empty and blood-stained bed.

24

HAYLEY

What if she's taken a turn for the worse? Or what if she's dead?

I hurtle along the corridor and a woman pushing a trolley between the curtained bays shouts something after me. Another nurse appears from one of the bays.

'My mother.' I shriek as I point back along the corridor. 'Where is she?' Oh God, what if something's happened and I wasn't even with her? How could I have left her all alone?

'She go scan.' The nurse points at her own head. 'You wait.' She now points back to the room I just came from.

I glance at my watch as I trudge back. Lance should be around ninety minutes away by now. If only Mum didn't have that head injury. Cuts, bruises and broken bones all heal easily enough but whatever's going on with her head, since the injury is unseen and unknown, it could be far more sinister.

As I retake my seat by her empty bed, Carl enters my head. *Carl.* I still need to get to the bottom of why he and Mum have been messaging. The police have taken her phone so will no doubt be asking questions about that message when they see it, especially in view of what's happened to her. Not that *he* could be something to do with it, of course.

I tug my phone back out. There's still nothing from him. He hasn't replied to my text, nor has he tried calling back, which is unusual, given the messages we've been sending since Dad's funeral.

He'll have finished work round about now and if I know him correctly, he'll be in the pub. Normally, it would have been *our* pub, The Dales Inn. He and Dad got on so well – too well. I liked this, at least to start with, but after we'd split up, I was incensed that Dad continued to see him and get along with him. Mum was even more furious. After all, his allegiance should have been with me, his daughter. Still that's all water under the bridge now and I prefer that we're getting on again. However, I'm unsure of whether it will ever lead anywhere.

I try to call him again. There's still no reply. But then my phone beeps with a Messenger message.

> Sorry Hayley, can't talk right now. What's up? x

> I need to know why you and my mother have been messaging each other.

> Is that what she said?

> I've seen part of your message on her lock screen.

Shit. No sooner have I hit send that I want to retract my message but it's too late. I've given Carl far too much information in that last one. If there's *anything* I should know, admitting to him from the off that I've only seen part of that message gives him carte blanche to lie through his teeth and make up a story about it. And he was always good at that.

> It's between me and your Mum, Hayles. No need for you to get involved.

So there is something I should know then.

> Well, my mother's having a brain scan – checking for internal bleeding after she was found unconscious on some rocks. So it's between me and you now.

My phone bursts into life with a Messenger call. Of course, it's him.

'You're joking, aren't you?'

'Oh yeah. Like I'd joke about something like this.'

'Where are you?'

'Where do you think I am? At the hospital of course.'

'How long have you been there?

'What does that matter?' My voice falters. 'A couple of hours.'

'What happened?'

'That's what the police are trying to find out. They've got her phone so if your messages are hiding *anything* from me, you might as well come out with it now.'

'Of course I'm not hiding *anything*. Look Hayles, it sounds as though you've got enough going on without worrying about a bit of messaging.'

'I'm going to find out what's been going on sooner or later so I'd rather hear it from you.' Even though I'm angry with him, it's still a comfort to hear his voice from back home. I feel so alone right now.

He falls quiet for a moment, evidently he's choosing his words. 'OK, do you remember when I came over to the three of you when you were looking at the aftermath of the fire?'

'Vaguely. That time's pretty much a blur.' I scrunch my eyes against the image of the still smouldering pub as it floods my mind. 'Didn't Mum tell you to do one, or words to that effect?'

'Something like that – and I can't say I blamed her. It was awful timing.'

'Erm, yes. What was so important you had to bother her *then*?'

'It was to do with some money your dad owes me.'

'He's dead, Carl.' As if *anyone* needs reminding. My tone of voice sounds dead as well. Surely Carl hasn't been hassling Mum for whatever *Dad* owed him? But his use of the word *owes* is ominous.

'I thought—'

'Hang on – is this why you've been back in touch with *me* since his funeral?' A wave of anger crashes over me. 'To use me to get to my mother?'

'Of course not, it's not like that at all. Being in touch with you is separate from anything else – but yes, I *have* been trying to get what she owes me.'

'She owes you *nothing* – she never has.' I jump up from my seat. 'And she's got *nothing* to give you in any case, do you hear me?'

'She must have *something* to have got you both on holiday to Turkey.' With a comment like this, the old Carl's back. Not that he'll have ever truly gone away.

'I paid for it, you heartless bastard. Didn't you just hear what I said? Her brain's being scanned to see whether she's going to live, die or have brain damage for the rest of her life, yet all you care about is her money, which once again, I'll reiterate that she *hasn't* got.'

A nurse pokes her head around the curtain of the room I'm pacing up and down in. She gives me a quizzical look. I raise my hand. 'I'm sorry. I'll stop.'

She won't understand what I've just said but should have picked up the drop in my voice and the apologetic gesture. I shouldn't be shouting, not in here of all places.

'Look it's not like that at all, Hayley – I'm sorry. I didn't mean to upset you. It sounds like you've enough to contend with.'

'And what's *your* mother got to do with all this?' I drop back into my seat.

'What are you on about?' He sounds puzzled. But not as puzzled as I am.

'Like I said, I saw your message – saying my mum hadn't responded to you *or* your mother – what's all that about?'

He pauses for too long before replying. Long enough to be concocting something. 'It's nothing.' He's lying, I'm certain of it. 'She's just been backing me up, that's all.' His voice has a slight shake. Another sign he's lying. I know all the signs of deceit from the legal training I've done. And if I was sitting straight opposite him now, he'd be avoiding my eye too.

'Then you threatened her, Carl. You said she'd left you with no choice other than to do *something*. Then the message cut off on her screen. What's going on?'

Some might say that I've done well to remember the wording of the message, especially with the stress I'm currently under, but the words have etched themselves into my brain. A cold feeling creeps over me as he remains deathly silent.

'Answer me, Carl? I need you to tell me what's going on. Or should I be telling this to the police?'

'OK then.' He lets out a long breath. 'I hadn't wanted to get into this but the threat I made to her was...'

'Was *what*?'

'That I was going to tell you what she's been up to.'

'*Been up to*? What are you talking about?' Oh God, what the hell am I about to hear? I know from her carry on with Jay that Mum likes younger men but surely she wouldn't be having anything to do with my ex-boyfriend of all people?

'Your mum's been hounding me, Hayles.'

'What do you mean?' Do I really want to hear this?

'She got wind of me and you being back in touch and clearly hasn't liked it.'

I let my breath go, feeling almost relieved at his reply. 'How's she found out?' Thank goodness it isn't what I thought it could be. But why hasn't she said anything?

'Maybe you've left your phone lying about or perhaps you've told someone who's then told her.'

'There's only Georgia who knows anything.' Bloody Georgia. Wait until I see her. Just because we've been friends since primary school and she knows Mum as well as she does, doesn't give her the right to go reporting on me. Georgia's already had a go at me for letting Carl back into my life. 'Hang on, even if she *does* know, it still doesn't explain why *your* Mum's involved in anything.'

'She intercepted one of your mum's nasty messages and took it upon *herself* to get involved. Especially since she knew about the outstanding money.'

'What do you mean, *get involved*?' Great. This is all I need.

'My mum rang your mum, warning her that unless she came to an arrangement about the money I was owed, she'd be forced to let you know how she's been interfering in your life and sending me messages.'

'I can't believe she hasn't said anything.' I look at the patch of blood on the sheet. My *mother's* blood. Evidently, she'll stop at nothing to keep Carl and I apart but I still can't believe *his* mother's got involved as well.

'She's just trying to protect you. But honestly, Hayles, she was the same when we were together last year – perhaps if she'd just let us be, we might have been alright.'

'Our *former* relationship...' I place an emphasis on the word so Carl doesn't get any ideas — 'and any money my dad might have owed to you before he died are two completely separate things.'

'I know that.' He sighs. 'But somehow it's all become one big toxic mess.'

'I just can't understand why your Mum's involved. I've never even met the woman.'

'I'm her son, aren't I? I'd already told her about some of the grief your mum had given me and she'll have been upset about it. I also owe her a fortune in board and other money I've borrowed from her before I got this new job. So it's in her interests that Debra pays Bryn's debt too.'

'It's *not* my mother's responsibility to pay my dad's debts.' I slap my hand onto my leg as I say the word *not*. 'What did he owe you money for anyway?'

'Just some work I did for him when I was on my uppers.'

'What work?' Part of me can't believe we're having this conversation when things with Mum are so much in the balance, but the other part of me welcomes the distraction while she's having her scan.

'Look, let's put all that to one side for now.' He must read my mind. 'All that matters is your Mum.'

'I know.'

'What have they told you? Is she going to be OK?' I soften at his change of discussion. Even though he and Mum have been having their differences, he still cares that she's going to be alright, even if it is more for *my* sake.

'I really don't know.' My voice is small. 'It all depends on the results of the brain scan they've taken her down for. Whatever's happened has made a right mess of her.'

'Is she conscious?'

'She's been totally out of it since they found her.' My voice shakes. 'I just feel so helpless. I've no idea what happened – I mean, how the hell she's got the injuries like she has from going for a *swim*.'

'What do you mean?'

'Well, she's covered in cuts and bruises, she's got several broken bones, but it's the head thing, whatever it turns out to be, which is the most cause for concern.' The vision of Mum's blue eyes, as unblinking as a lifeless fish fills my mind. 'They tried shining a torch in her eyes before and she apparently wasn't responding like she should be. It's why they've taken her for a scan.'

He falls quiet. He won't have a clue what to say. It was the same with everyone when Dad died. People were no doubt worried about saying the wrong thing, therefore they didn't say anything at all.

'You still there?'

'Is anyone taking care of you at the hospital?' Carl's voice is soft.

Despite everything, I suddenly wish, more than anything in the world that Carl was here with me. I could lean into his shoulder and feel the strength of his arms around me. It's crazy, I know it is, but the messages I've had from him over the last couple of months show that he still cares about me. And with *him*, I could always be myself, I never had to pretend. Mum might not have been able to stand the sight of him but Dad thought he was great, which surely must count for something.

'I'm more concerned about Mum right now.' I rub at the side of my arm, almost trying to comfort myself. 'I'm worried she might not come through this.' Now I've said the words out loud, my breath begins to come faster. 'I've already been told to prepare for the worst.'

'You sound remarkably calm, considering.'

'I'm just numb, to be honest,' I reply. 'It really hasn't hit me yet. Besides, I've got to stay strong for my mum, haven't I?'

'I'm here for you if you need me. All you've got to do is ring. At any time. I'll have my phone beside me even when I go to sleep later.'

Sleep. What a wonderful escape that would be right now. I'm veering between exhaustion after not falling asleep until dawn after what happened to me last night, and a nervous high alert as I await news from Mum's scan. Part of me would prefer just to wait in blissful ignorance. *No news is good news* as she's always said.

'Are you going to be alright?' He sounds like he's about to hang up. Part of me doesn't really want him to.

'I'll have to be. It won't do anyone any good if I fall apart, will it?'

'I'm proud of you,' he says. 'And your Dad would be too. I just wish I was there to support you.'

'Thank you.' I sniff. 'So do I.' I can say this, knowing there isn't a cat in hell's chance that could ever be true. In the duration of our relationship, he was always skint. We didn't even have a weekend away at the seaside, let alone a sunshine holiday together.

'I'd better go and ask if there's been any developments yet,' I tell him.

'Just remember what I said,' he says. 'I'm here for you. Just like I always have been.'

His words shouldn't warm me, but they do.

But right now, all that matters is my mother.

25

HAYLEY

I SIT at the side of the trolley, watching the clock as another hour crawls by. My backside is numb from sitting here for so long and I'm parched. I should find a drink from somewhere but I'm scared to move in case someone comes back with news. I scroll around on my phone to distract myself. Looking at the happy holiday photos of others and pictures of friends and colleagues enjoying their nights out leaves me cold. I want to tell the world of the danger my mother is in but then I'll only be fielding questions and having to give news updates to everyone back home, neither of which I have the energy for. There'll be time for all that when I know more of what's happening.

'Is there any news on my mother yet?' A nurse frowns at me as I point at the empty trolley, signalling that she doesn't understand a word I'm saying as she scurries along the corridor. I want to scream in frustration.

'How the hell am I to find out what's going on with Mum when barely no one speaks any English here?'

This is absolute hell. Then my phone beeps.

> Thinking of you and here for you anytime. We're letting your dad's debt go. All that matters is you, and that your mum's alright. x

Carl *has* changed. Dad once said something along the lines of, *You don't know what you've got until it's gone,* and I think there's a lot of truth in this.

> Thanks. I'll keep you posted.

> I regret ever coming after her. Honestly, Hayles. I'm sorry.

> I appreciate you being there for me.

My phone beeps again but rather that it being Carl, it's Lance. Thank goodness. He must have landed.

> How's Mum?

> She's still wherever they've taken her for a scan so I'm not sure. She's been gone for ages. By the time you get here, we should know more.

> A scan for what?

> A brain scan. They need to check for fractures and bleeding.

> Oh my God. Tell me when you hear anything, won't you.'

> Of course I will. How long will you be?

> About an hour at least. I've still got to get through security. Do you want anything? Have you eaten?

Typical Lance. No matter what the incident, his thoughts never stray far from his belly.

> I couldn't eat a thing. Not until I know she's going to be alright.

> Have you asked someone what's going on?

> No one speaks any bloody English.

> Some one must. Just keep trying. I'll be there as quick as I can. Where are you when I get there?

> Still at the Emergency Room.

> Maybe you should try to find wherever they're supposed to be scanning her.

> Good idea. If I'm not here when you arrive, go there.

> See you soon, sis. Love you.

Tears burn at the back of my eyes. He only ever says this when the chips are really down in our family. Which has been a lot over the last year. But it's what I need to hear. If anything happens to Mum, my brother might be the only family I have left. I must stop thinking like this. Mum always manages to look on the positive side and so should I.

Thank goodness for Google. I discover that a CT scan is held within a Tomography Department, translating to Tomografi in Turkish.

Going down there is what I should have done in the first place –

I'm just not thinking straight tonight. Grabbing my bag, I stand from my chair and head along the corridor to the exit of the emergency room. Someone calls after me in Turkish, but I carry on walking. I'm off to find Mum and no one's going to stop me.

'Debra Ford,' I say to the woman behind the desk as I finally find where I'm supposed to be. 'You speak English?'

'A moment.' She leaves the desk, leaving me standing here like a lemon. I glance up at the board of entries – Mum's name's not on there. I hope I'm in the right place and that one of the medical staff isn't looking for me back at the Emergency Room with news.

The woman returns with a young-looking man, dressed in scrubs. This isn't a good sign at all.

'Are you her daughter?' His face is serious – deadly serious.

'Yes. Where's my mum? How is she?'

He points to a door. 'We prepare her for operation. She bleeds on her brain.'

'Oh my God.' I stumble back from him and lean against the wall. 'Can you...? Will she...?' I can hardly get my words out. 'Can I see her before you take her, just for a moment. Why did nobody tell me?'

'We're telling you now. And we need you to sign forms.'

This really isn't happening. I know what he means. The forms will be disclaimers in case anything goes wrong for her on the operating table. It can't – it just can't.

'Come with me please.'

I stand up straight and go after him. My head's swimming again as I try to keep up with him along the corridor towards a sign. I've no idea what it says.

'Sorry for your wait.' Another scrubbed up man says as I go in. 'We need sign then help your mum. She is bleeding on her brain and we need to clip and drain.' He makes a scissoring action with his fingers. Oh my God - as if this is even happening.

We're in a foreign country and my mother needs life saving surgery.

'Will she live?' This is all that matters. Also, will she even be herself afterwards? I remember her once saying that if she was ever in a situation where she'd have no quality of life, we should let her go. *After all,* she said, *if it were Sammy, we could put her to sleep. I'm only asking for the same dignity.*

But I thought that kind of decision would be years and years away when she's elderly and infirm. She's only fifty, no matter how much she moaned about feeling old. Dad would sometimes joke about how they were in the prime of their lives.

'We do our best,' he says. 'The team – they are very good. She's in best hands.'

'Can I see her?' A cloud crosses his face which says, *no, of course you can't.* 'Please! Just for a minute. My Dad died earlier this year. She's the only parent I have left.' I just want to give her a kiss and let her know I'm here – that Lance and I are waiting for her to be OK and to be brought back to us.

'For a minute.' He beckons and I follow him down another shiny white corridor and pushes the door into a room. He stands before her and I gasp at the sight that befalls me. I wish he could have warned me. Mum's now hooked up to far more monitors than she was when I last saw her, and laid on a larger trolley than the one in the emergency room. She looks small and vulnerable and all I want to do is protect her like she's always protected me. Tears prickle my eyes again.

'Can you leave us for a moment please?' I dart to her side.

'OK,' he says as I reach for my mother's hand and kiss it. I can't hold back the tears as I consider that this could be the final time I ever see her. No, Hayley, you can't think like this – you just can't, you need to be more like she is. You *have* to stay positive.

'I don't know what the hell's happened to you, Mum. But I *need* you to come out of this and be OK. Promise me you'll fight your hardest fight in there.' I kiss her hand again.

I stare at her, the bruising on her face seems to have come up even more than when I last saw her nearly ninety minutes ago. Lance is going to be in pieces when he sees her. I force another intrusive thought from my mind – *if* he sees her.

'They're going to fix you up and then you're going to heal and somehow, we'll all get back to normal again, I promise.'

Whatever *normal* is. When I consider how much we've endured as a family over the last few months, it turns my stomach.

Mum's hand is warm and limp within mine and I'd give anything for her to suddenly squeeze mine and reassure me that she'll be OK. 'Lance is in a taxi from the airport, he'll be with us soon. We're both here for you, Mum. We just need you to fight your hardest in there.'

'It is time now.' The doctor, surgeon, or whoever he is re-enters the room. I want to ask what the exact procedure is that they're planning and where on her brain her bleed is so I can Google it. But that's stupid – I'll only frighten myself and Lance even more if I know the ins and outs of it all. I want to ask what her chances are in there and what the chances are of any permanent damage. I want to ask how long she'll be here for afterwards. But I *have* to put my faith in them and just let them get on with making her better, what else can I do?

'You should go rest and eat,' another medic says, thrusting a pad of paper and a pen at me. 'You give number, we call you.'

I shake my head. 'I'm waiting right here,' I reply. 'And so is my brother when he arrives.'

26

HAYLEY

'Oh, Lance.' I fall into his arms as soon as he's ducked beneath the doorway of the family waiting room.

'You took some finding,' he pulls me closer. 'Where's Mum? I thought you were with her.'

I tug back from him and study his face, clearly happy to see me while also etched with concern. Everyone says we look alike with the same blue eyes and core-flicked fringe. I can't bear to blow his world apart. As if he hasn't been through enough. As if we haven't *both* been through enough.

'She's going to be alright, isn't she?' He lowers himself onto one of the plastic sofas once I've finished telling him what I know. Well, a very watered-down version of it. 'Course she will, she's as tough as old boots, our Mum. It's where you get it from, sis. Me, I'm just a jelly like Dad was.'

Lance's face darkens as he mentions him. We don't talk about Dad as much as we should – it's too painful. So many people will think he deserved to die after what he tried to do to Jay, but I spoke to him that day, only hours before the pub went up in flames. I might be the only person who knows how much pain he was in and how he wasn't thinking straight. I just wish I'd got more involved – made my effort with *him* rather than trying to reason with Jay.

'I honestly don't know, bro. Can I have some of that.' I reach for my brother's water bottle. 'I've drunk all I had.'

'What have they said about Mum?'

'The problem we've got is they don't speak proper English. All I know is that they're trying to stem and drain a brain bleed. So obviously, there's a chance of damage or....' My words fade out.

'Worse.' Lance stares at the floor, his face stony and his eyes wet. 'She can't die, Hayles, she just can't.'

'I know.' I reach for his arm, tears burning at the back of my own eyes too. 'They let me see her for a minute just before she went down to theatre and I reminded her how much we love her.'

'I wish I could have seen her.' Lance's voice wobbles. 'What if I never see her again?'

'I've ordered her that she's *got* to be alright. She was out of it, but I'm sure her eyes flickered when she heard my voice.'

I'm not going to tell Lance the extent of her injuries and how awful she looks. Not yet anyway, however when we're allowed to see her after she comes out of theatre, I'll have to warn him then.

If she comes out of theatre.

'What time is it, sis?' Lance opens his eyes from where he's scrunched up on the two seater sofa facing me, his gangly legs draped over one arm of it. 'I can't believe I dropped off?'

'Just for a few minutes,' I reply, lowering my voice. It's not as if I'm going to wake anyone by speaking in my normal voice but it feels like the respectful thing to do at this hour. 'But it's OK – I bet you're knackered.' I've tried to close my eyes too but every time I do, all I see is Mum. She's standing behind the bar, laughing at some gossip a customer's told her. Or she's putting her face on while I sit on her bed and we chat away, her moaning about her crows feet and sagging jawline. No matter how many times I've told her she's beautiful, she's never believed me.

I've curled into a foetal position on the sofa while Lance has been asleep, talking to her inside my mind like I did when she was late picking me up as a kid. *Keep fighting, Mum,* I've told her. *You've so much to live for. We've had such a hard time as a family, but it's all going to get better once we get through this.* I haven't let myself cry since Lance arrived – I'm just trying to keep it together for him. There's no need to cry – not yet – not when there's still everything we can hope for.

'I managed to doze off on the plane as well,' he replies. 'I never dreamt we'd still be waiting for news at half past four in the morning. It must be serious if they're operating at this time of night.'

'I know.' I reach for the jug of water the nurse has thankfully brought in and fill one of the plastic cups.

'I don't want to say this, sis, but maybe we need to prepare ourselves. She's been in there for ages.'

'Nope – she's going to be just fine.' I hoist myself up to a seated position.

'I just don't understand how she's managed to get such an awful head injury while *swimming*,' he continues.

'I know. I was saying the same thing to...' My voice trails off. I nearly said *Carl* but if Lance knew I'd been talking to him, he'd hit the roof. He wouldn't believe he's changed, not for a second, and would dismiss any arguments I might put forward about people deserving a second chance. 'One of the police officers,' I add.

'I take it they're trying to find out what happened to Mum?'

'Of course they are.' I draw my knees into my chest. 'Look bro, I need to tell you more of what's been going on. The full story this time.' I do need to talk to him – I can no longer cope with all this on my own.

'I think you'd better had.' He stiffens as he looks at me and I feel bad for not telling him in the first place.

Lance's face changes from sorrow to anger as I regale the last day or so. From Mum's *real* reason for being here in Bodrum, to me being abducted from the Turkish Baths and thrown into the back of a van. And now, to *this*.

'Oh my God, those bastards didn't *do* anything to you, did they?' Lance looks as distraught as he did before I managed to calm him down an hour ago. Before sleep rescued him for a while.

'That was the first thing Mum asked too.' The memory of the concern that swam in her eyes makes me want to sob. 'But no, they didn't hurt me. That doesn't mean I didn't think they were going to. If I'm honest, I thought it was curtains for me. I was amazed when they suddenly let me go.'

'Did they say *why* they'd taken you. I mean, it seems really odd – you're fresh off a plane from England just about and you're randomly dragged out of some baths place and locked in the back of a Turkish motor. Then they suddenly let you go?'

I shake my head. 'They didn't say *anything*. I don't even think they spoke any English. They just dumped me out at the side of the road.'

'Did you not get their number plate?'

'To be honest, I was so relieved to be out that I just ran for it. I kept thinking they'd made a mistake and were going to come back for me.

'Then what? You went to the police, I take it?'

'I just wanted Mum.' Tears are rolling down my cheeks at the memory of how she wrapped me in her arms when she saw me. 'I managed to flag down a taxi and get back to the hotel.'

'How far's the hotel from *here*?'

'I've no idea. It took about half an hour to drive here from where they found Mum and it was about forty minutes from the airport but I'm not sure which direction.'

'So...' I can literally see his brain ticking over. 'You *have* told the police what happened to you today, haven't you?'

'I have *now*.' I wrap my arms around myself, comforted by the temporary heat from my hands against the tops of my arms in this chilly air-conditioned room. Surely, it doesn't need to be turned up this high. Not for people like us as we sit around, often alone, waiting for some positive dead-of-night news. 'The officer seemed to think there was a good chance that me being grabbed and what's happened to Mum is linked. They were starting their inquiry with the Turkish Baths.'

'Are you telling me they're thinking Mum's *accident* wasn't an accident after all?'

'I really don't know yet. No one's telling us a thing, are they? But that's not all—'

There's a tapping at the door and one of the men in scrubs from earlier puts his head around it. Lance and I jump to our feet at the same time.

'Please sit down.' His expression is impossible to read.

We drop like stones back to where we came from. My head swoons after the sudden movement.

'Is there some news?' All colour has drained from Lance's face. It will have from mine as well.

'She has come through,' he replies. There's no hint of anything softening in his expression as he continues. 'It was a success but a long way still to go.'

'Where is she?'

'She will be taken to ICU.'

'Is she going to be alright?'

He shakes his head. 'It's too early. We observe. We see.'

'Can we see her please?' A tear splashes down Lance's cheek. 'I've just flown from the UK. I need to see my mum.'

'We've been waiting for a bed,' he says. 'She needs rest. One has just come. You go home and sleep. We will call if there is a change. She will be unconscious for a while.'

The translator told me there's a desperate shortage of ICU beds in Turkey. For Mum to be getting moved to one, things must be as serious as they get. I had an awful feeling as soon as Mum was taken for her scan that her head injury was going to be something sinister. And for a bed to be available in Intensive Care, someone must have died for the space to have been made. I feel as gloomy as a midwinter funeral.

I think of the family who've just lost someone, praying it's not about to be mine and Lance's turn shortly.

'She's come through the operation, sis. That's got to be good news.' Lance rests his hand on my back. He's so much more gentle than he normally would be. Usually we're making fun of each other and seeing who can give the best dead arm.

'Will you take good care of her if we leave for a bit?' The thought of some tea, a shower and curling up for an hour in the darkness of the hotel room suddenly feels inviting, 'We'll sleep and then we'll be back.'

'I don't want to leave her, Hayles.' Lance's lip wobbles in the way I used to think was really cute when he was a little boy. 'Maybe one of us could go and the other could stay.'

'We're both done in, bro. Look, even if we just get an hour to rest and a shower, it'll make all the difference.'

'But—'

'We'll get a shower—' My voice is firm and I have to admit that I sound a bit like Mum. 'We'll have some food and we'll come straight back. We can be here for her when she wakes up. She's going to be out of it for some time yet.'

'OK.' Lance gets back to his feet. 'I guess she's going to need us more in a few hours than she will right now.'

If the surgeon understands any of our conversation, he doesn't let on. But the look on his face which is bordering on sympathetic suggests I'm deluding myself.

27

TINA

'I THOUGHT I told you not to answer calls or messages from *her*.' As soon as Carl leaves the bathroom, I'm lying in wait for him.

'What are you on about?' He frowns.

'I heard you last night.'

I had to stop myself from barging in on him and demanding to know what was going on. But I didn't want to sleep on the back of an argument. I'm away from that sort of thing for a few days. I do enough crying myself to sleep at home.

'Hayley's mother's in a really bad way by the sounds of it.' He leans up against the wall, squinting in the morning sun. I wish we were just here to go and laze in the heat all day. A proper holiday – sadly a luxury not afforded to people like us. 'I wasn't going to ignore her, was I? She's here – in a foreign country and she's totally on her own.'

I'm not sure what I can see in his face but where Hayley's concerned, he appears to have gone soft again. This is all I need.

'She ignored *you* for long enough, didn't she, and why are you so bothered about Debra all of a sudden?'

'I'm not – but Hayley—'

'Do you need reminding about everything Debra said about

you? Even to me, on that train – a complete stranger as far as we both knew at the time?'

'Alright, Mum.'

'It was clearly a blatant lie that she's got no money – she's been having us both on if you ask me.'

'She was having a CT scan on her brain when I spoke to Hayley. It sounds as serious as it could be.' He stands up straight and threads his head through the t-shirt he's carried with him out of the bathroom.

'So I gathered from what you were saying to her.' I resist the urge to mimic him. *I'm always here for you,* he said. You don't say that to an ex if there isn't still *something* going on between you.

'Debra's really got to you, hasn't she, Mum? I thought you'd be more upset about where she's ended up?' He looks at me in the same way his father does. Like he's trying to read me.

'Do they have any idea of what's happened to put her there yet?' I rub at my head. I had a terrible night's sleep and I don't sleep well as it is – between listening out for a husband who rarely comes home, coupled with dealing with the ghastly menopause. Last night, I had even less chance of sleeping.

Carl shakes his head. 'As far as they know, she had some kind of accident while swimming in that bay. No one saw, no one heard a thing – Hayley said it was early in the morning when she left.'

'Well perhaps, as a woman on her own, she was asking for trouble, swimming alone, in a foreign country, early in the morning.' Blimey, if I said this sort of thing at work, I'd be lynched for it. 'I think you should watch yourself around Hayley though,' I continue. 'I can see trouble ahead if you don't.'

'I didn't expect to be suckered in by her again if I'm honest. But I am, Mum and I can't help it if I still have feelings for her.' At least he has the grace to look apologetic. 'It's a complete mess, isn't it?'

'We'll have to sit tight until there's some news and we know more about what's been going on. But in the meantime, we can't say we haven't tried *everything.*'

'I'm off for a walk.' Carl picks up his phone and slides it into his back pocket. 'I need to clear my head.'

'Wait. I'll come with you – I could do with getting out of this apartment.' I look around at the dingy four walls which are beginning to squash me between them.

'I meant on my own.' At least he looks awkward which is more than he used to. 'I could do with working out how to handle things with Hayley.'

'I've told you how to handle things – stay well clear. OK then, I know when I'm not wanted.'

'It's not what you think. Honestly, Mum, I just can't think straight.'

'It's OK. Look, I'll head down to the mall and do some window-shopping.' A ripple of bitterness snakes up my spine. 'Since that's all I can afford to do until *something* gets sorted.' I give him a loaded look. He knows as well as I do that we can't go on like this for much longer.

My sandals slap against the pavement as I make my way down to the mall. It's boiling already so I won't stay out in the heat for long. I burn to a crisp far too easily since I'm not used to it. It'll be because I've managed to finish up with a man who doesn't want to walk to the end of the street with me, let alone take me on holiday. And he thinks I'm going to roll over and let them force me from my home. So I've been left with no choice other than to join forces with my son like this. It's my only hope of raising some money to fight my corner.

A man doffs his hat as I pass him on the harbour, saying something to me with a smile. I think he's wishing me a good morning. Is it really? How can it be?

Debra's face sweeps into my mind. I got to know her more in

that couple of hours on the train than I've got to know most of the neighbours who've lived on my street for the past twenty years.

I could hardly believe it when I discovered she was the mother of a girl Carl had been involved with. As I played back everything she'd said about him, every nasty last word when I put the pieces together a couple of days later, I knew my time would come to take back some of what I deserve. What Carl deserves.

No matter what he might be thinking and feeling, *I've* never felt guilty about putting the squeeze on Debra Ford – not once.

28

HAYLEY

I'D GIVE anything to sleep. To escape from this fresh hell that we've been sucked into, even just for a couple of hours. Really, I'd love to get on a plane, return to the UK and get away from the darkness that's wrapped itself around Mum and I since we got here and for everything to be as it was.

The crickets might be happily chirping beyond this room, the days might be long and filled with sunshine, but the hole that's opened up inside me since my mother was found on those rocks is a gaping void, one that won't be filled unless she wakes up and they tell me she's going to get better.

It's no good. I can't lie here any longer. I sit up straight and look across at the sleeping form of my brother in Mum's bed. I have no idea how he can sleep so peacefully with all that's going on. He was the same when Dad died. My nights were haunted by the memory of the fire crew carrying that charred body from the pub, not realising at the time that it was my poor dad. The stench lingered in my nostrils for days – sometimes, even now, the memory of that smell catches me off guard. I often ruminate what might have been going through Dad's mind when he realised how trapped he was in the flat inside the pub, whereas

Lance, whilst he was as devastated as I was, still managed to eat and sleep as normal. I've only just got myself back together after it all.

And now this.

I reach for my phone yet again. We've been back at our hotel for several hours and there's still been no word from the hospital or the police. I'd ring them but there's the language barrier to contend with. We just need to wait, I know we do.

Messenger, however, is another story and is showing five messages – all from Carl.

> I can't sleep since we spoke. Can't stop thinking about you. xx

What the hell's that supposed to mean? If he thinks I'm giving him a second thought while Mum's in the state she's in, he's deluded.

> Any news on your Mum yet? xx

> Remember I'm here for you. Ring me if you need to. xx

> I managed to drop off – just woken up – just wondering how you are and how your Mum's doing?? xx

> Let me know. xx

It's nice that he cares so much but unnerving to get so many messages when he knows what's going on with me. I won't reply yet – there's nothing I can say anyway. Not until I get some news.

I flick the kettle switch. I'm not sure I'll be able to stomach any coffee but I need *something* to keep me going.

'Lance, wake up, will you? We have to get back to the hospital.'

'Umph, what—' He springs up. 'What do you mean? What's happened? Has Mum woken up?'

'I wish.' My eyes fall on her scribbled note from yesterday. If only I'd been awake when she left it. I'd have stopped her from going out on her own. I'd have gone with her and everything would have been OK then. 'No – I want to ring them but I won't be able to make myself understood.'

'How will going in there be any different? We still won't be able to understand much.' He frowns. 'That surgeon spoke a bit of English but the nurses barely speak a word.'

'At least if we're face to face, we can use signs and Google Translate like I had to do with the coastguard. A couple of times I got him to type his replies into my phone when I couldn't make out what he was trying to say.'

'I don't suppose there's any food on offer here, Hayles?'

'Typical.' I give him a playful push as he passes me. 'Just go out there, past the pool and turn left, and there's the breakfast buffet.'

'Right, I'll just grab some fruit or something then.' He pulls some shorts from his bag and steps into them. 'I'll bring you something back, shall I? Or are you coming with me?'

'I don't think I could eat a thing, bro.' My stomach's churning like a cement mixer. I hope to God that we get some positive news today. I don't know how we'll cope if things get any worse. 'Take my room key and tell them what's happened to Mum. Make sure you tell them you're my brother or they might send you packing.'

'You need to eat, sis – I'll grab you a pastry. Mum's gonna need us to be strong when she comes round, not empty, knackered wrecks.'

'I know.' Tears stab at the backs of my eyes as I subconsciously force the word *if* she comes around, from my vocabulary.

As the door clicks behind him, I quickly dress and gulp down some water. Its chill slides to my stomach but helps me to feel less nauseous. I check my phone again, and check the ringer volume is turned up for the fifth time since I got out of bed. Of course it is. I start making a coffee but the smell turns me off even as I spoon the granules into the cup.

'Come on, Lance.' I drum my fingers on the worktop. We've been gone too long and need to get back there. We've had some rest, we're getting some food but we need to be at Mum's side when she wakes up. She's *got* to wake up.

I jump as there's a tapping at the door and rush to open it. It can't be Lance already. Besides, I gave him my room key. But standing there instead is Christina, the hotelier, a police officer and another woman.

'This is who you're looking for,' Christina says. Her gaze softens as she looks at me. 'Your brother's just told me about your mum.'

'I'm Mennan Ceri,' says the woman, gesturing to herself before nodding to the man at her side. 'And this is Law Enforcement Officer Zarif. I'm an independent translator and—'

'What happened to the other two?'

'They're off duty now so we've taken over.'

'With what? All of it?'

'Yes – *your* abduction the night before last, *and* how your mother came to be on those rocks in the bay yesterday. Can we come in?'

Christina reaches around the police officer and squeezes my arm. 'I really hope she's going to be alright. Please just say if there's anything we can do to help.'

It dawns on me that as someone who can understand both Turkish and English, there might be something Christina can do, but right now, I'm mainly interested in what the police are here for.

'Thanks,' I say. 'I promise I'll let you know.'

'I'll leave you to it for now,' she replies.

I open the door wider. 'Please, come in. Sit down.' I move the pile of clothes Mum left on the sofa to one side and perch on the edge of my bed facing the man and the woman. 'Do you know if there's any news from the hospital yet? My mother was going from theatre into intensive care at five o'clock this morning. And they sent us away to get some rest.'

Mennan says something to Officer Zarif, who replies to her in Turkish.

'The police were in touch with the hospital an hour ago and there was no change in her condition – she's described as being in an induced coma to give her body the chance to recover. But she's being closely monitored and they'll be in touch straight away if there's any change.'

The police officer says something again, speaking at length until not knowing what he's saying becomes unbearable.

'Officer Zarif has asked me to tell you that a blank has been drawn at the Turkish Baths you told the police about,' Mennan eventually relays. 'The only CCTV is at the front entrance, and in the reception area, but as you mentioned, you left the building through a rear entrance where there's no coverage. And the people who work there are telling us nothing.'

'What about the staff member who showed me in and to the cubicle?' She seemed alright – I'd go as far to say that I trusted her.

'She's maintaining that you went into a cubicle to undress and then just disappeared when she returned for you. It was assumed you'd changed your mind and left.'

'What about CCTV of the van? There must be *something*. It felt like it was driving around for ages.' I'll never forget how sick I felt in the back of it as I was tossed around like a sock in a tumble drier.

The interpreter and the officer once again confer.

'Without you being able to tell us the make, model, colour or registration of the vehicle, there's little to go on. However, footage in the surrounding streets of the baths is being examined.'

'What about the boat Jay Manningham is supposed to be staying on? Or the beach bar he's working at?'

Again, they confer.

'No one has heard his name despite the extensive enquiries that have been conducted, both after your mother was admitted to hospital yesterday and first thing this morning.'

I stare back at her, resisting the urge to beat my fists against the wall in frustration.

'We really need more information,' she continues. 'Particularly if your mother knows an exact location where we might find this man.'

'But she's not in a position to tell you anything, is she?'

Lance bursts in. 'What's going on? Have you caught up with him yet?' He's got croissant crumbs down his top and his hair's on end. My lovely, dear brother. I'm so relieved he's here and I'm not facing this all on my own.

'And you are?'

'Lance Ford. I'm Hayley's brother.' He gestures towards me.

'This is a police officer and an interpreter,' I explain.

'Debra's son?' Mennan raises an eyebrow.

'Yes.'

'Unfortunately,' Mennan begins. 'We're only here to say that the police haven't found *anything* so far, but that doesn't mean we're not continuing to try. Obviously, if your mother pulls through—'

'*When* she pulls through,' Lance corrects her.

'Sorry. All I'm saying is that your mother should be able to tell us more than we can uncover ourselves, and we'll have more of a chance of being able to question this Jay Manningham then.'

Officer Zarif says something to her.

'Would you like a lift to the hospital?' Mennan turns from him and back to us. 'We'll come in with you and see how she's doing, if that's alright?'

'That's really kind of you.' I brighten somewhat, despite the awfulness of the situation. As I found at the start of this year, people are nearly always happy to help. 'I'd also be hugely grateful if you'd be able to take five minutes to help relay whatever the hospital staff try to tell us about Mum's condition.'

I can only pray it's positive news.

29

HAYLEY

THE STENCH of antiseptic hits me as soon as we walk in. I've managed to get half a croissant down which Lance brought from the breakfast buffet for me. It threatens to reappear as we follow Mennan and Officer Zarif along the sunny white corridor. At least they seem to know where they're going. I was in too much of a daze when we were here a few hours ago to take much notice, and of course, I can't understand a word displayed on any of the signs.

'You need to prepare yourself, bro.' I reach for my brother's arm as I remember that he hasn't seen the state of Mum yet. 'She's in a bit of a mess.'

'I'm prepared.' But his voice shakes despite the bravado of his words. 'Don't worry, I'll keep it together in there.'

'You don't have to.' I squeeze his arm. 'I've got you.'

'We've got each other,' he replies, linking arms with me as we're buzzed into the intensive care unit.

'Can you do the talking when we get to the desk?' I turn to Mennan. 'And then relay to us any information they give us on our mother's condition.'

'Of course.' She smiles which puts me slightly more at ease. What we're asking her to do will be above the call of her duty. She's probably only paid to liaise between us and the police. 'You'll no doubt have to authorise me to do so.'

As we get to the end of the corridor, an alarm wails through the air. Several doctors are crowded around someone's bed. They're clearly in trouble. Lance grips my arm even tighter.

It takes a moment or two for me to realise what's happening. 'Mum,' I screech as I surge forward, breaking free of Lance. 'That's our mum.' I shriek even louder as a nurse darts from behind the desk and pulls me back from the door. 'Please, just let me through.'

Another nurse joins her in steering me away, and they jabber at me in Turkish.

'You're both to wait in there.' Mennan points towards a room. 'I'll find out what's happening and follow you in.' I don't know how her voice can be so steady and calm but then it's not her mother literally fighting for her life. She heads towards one of the nurses and Officer Zarif goes after her.

I can't move. When I try, I find that I'm frozen to the spot, as another three medics zoom past us, wheeling a machine on a trolley between them. One of them pulls the blinds down in the room containing my mother.

'What's going on?' Lance clutches at my arm again. Even though I can no longer see anything, I still can't tear my eyes away. 'I thought she'd be OK. They said she just needed to rest.'

'So did I.' I come to at the sound of my brother's voice. 'Look, Mennan will find out what's going on. We'll do what they said.' Big sister mode kicks in and I realise I need to get him away from watching this. 'Let's wait in that room like they told us. She'll be OK.' I steer him towards the door.

'She didn't look OK to me.' Tears are rolling down his cheeks as he paces the floor in the family room we've been sent to. It's identical to the one we waited in last night. Grey with plastic sofas, a low table and a box of tissues. I yank a couple from the box.

'She's a fighter.' I thrust them at him. 'We've got to hold onto that.'

'What if she dies? Oh Hayles, we're going to be orphans.' He barely pauses for breath.

'You listen to me.' I grab each of his shoulders and give him a gentle shake. 'If me and you lose hope for her, what's left?' I tilt his chin so his pain-filled eyes meet mine. 'She'll pull through this – I know she will.'

'I hope you're right.' His voice is small and wobbly. My stomach's in knots as I take in a long breath to try and calm myself down. I need to know what's going on. We both jump as the door opens and Mennan bursts in.

'Officer Zarif's just on his radio with the station,' she explains. 'It seems something may have come in.'

'Never mind that.' Lance's voice is suddenly stronger and sharper. 'What's happened to Mum? Is she...' The words trail off. It's as if he can't bear to say what might come next.

'She's taken a turn for the worse,' Mennan explains. 'They're just trying to stabilise her and will be along to see us as soon as possible.'

'What's happened? What do you mean, *a turn for the worse*?' I really can't cope with much more of this. Tears are sliding down my cheeks now.

Lance throws his arms around me. 'What was it you said only a couple of minutes ago? She'll pull through this, right?'

'There's every reason to believe that,' Mennan says, her steady voice an oasis of calm in our swirling world. 'This is a reputable hospital and they'll do everything they can.'

But I can't quell the bubbling dread in my stomach, no matter how hard anyone tries to reassure me.

We sit in silence for a few moments until Officer Zarif taps on the door and says something to Mennan. Normally I'd be quizzing her about their efforts to find Jay but I can't focus on anything other than Mum right now.

'Just give me a couple of minutes.' She gets to her feet. 'I'll be straight back in to let you know what he tells me.'

Lance and I remain silent and rooted to our seats, facing each other across the table while they talk outside. There are no more words of comfort, not until we know anything with a degree of certainty. We've just got to trust. Trust Mum to fight, trust the staff to know what they're doing and trust God to look *after her.*

God. I've been too busy to allow him to figure in my life properly since childhood but right now, well, I'm willing to do or try *anything.*

I squeeze my eyes together and start begging in my head, *please let my mother be alright, please let her get through this, I'll do anything, just please, please, look after her and bring her back to us.*

I don't know how many minutes pass but fresh tears are bulging at my eyes as the door opens again. Lance darts to my side and Mennan and Officer Zarif face us on the sofa opposite.

'They've stabilised your mother,' Mennan says, relief etched into her smile. 'She's got a way to go but she's holding on.'

'Thank God.' It's Lance's turn to let out a long breath. 'What happened?'

'They tried bringing her off the ventilator,' she replies. 'A little too soon, it would seem. Everything dropped, from what I can gather, her heart rate, her blood pressure, her oxygen levels. That's why the crash team were called. She needs more time to recover before they can take her off it.'

'But she *will* recover, won't she?' I can hardly get my words out.

'I didn't realise she was on a *ventilator,*' says Lance.

'It's just to allow her to rest. That's what the nurse just told me. They're going to keep a close eye on her for a few more hours and then bring her off it more gradually next time.'

'I thought you said they knew what they were doing?' I point at Mennan, unable to keep the anger out of my voice. 'That this was one of the best hospitals?'

'It really is,' she replies. 'And we'll help you keep in touch with what's going on with language being such a barrier, but there's something else besides this.' She looks at Officer Zarif who nods. Lance and I exchange glances. What now?

'Our police colleagues have finally located Jay Manningham,' she begins.

'They have? Where?'

'We matched a photograph of him to his beach bar,' she replies. 'He was taken to the station around an hour ago.'

It's nothing short of a miracle that Mum and I had the chance to discuss Jay after I escaped from that van. Without that, I'd never have been able to point the police in his direction. It's also a miracle that I managed to get the truth out of her and discover what she was *really* doing here in Bodrum. It turned out to be the last conversation I would have with Mum – no, I mustn't think like this. I'll have many, many more conversations with her. Just as soon as she gets better.

'And?' Lance doesn't take his eyes off Mennan.

'Are you familiar with someone by the name of Carl Webb?'

'Yes.' A peculiar sensation crawls over me. What the hell would Carl have to do with anything that's going on here?

'We've been informed by Jay Manningham that Carl Webb is the person we need to speak to.'"

'What are you on about?' A cloud crosses Lance's face.

'It's been alleged that not only is he responsible for your sister being abducted,' – she gestures in my direction, – 'But he's also responsible for what's happened to your mother.'

'He can't be – he's in England.'

'Did Jay tell you this?' Lance looks from me back towards Mennan.

'Jay's trying to deflect the blame from himself,' I tell her. 'He'll have given you a name out of thin air just to throw you off *his* scent. Is he still at the police station?'

'For now,' Mennan replies. I can't imagine it's much different here than it is in England. They'll need something more to charge Jay with than just *me* telling them that he's involved.

'So Carl Webb—' she begins.

'Carl being involved wouldn't make any sense,' I continue. 'Like I just said, he's at home in England.'

'Unless he's arranged something from there,' Lance chips in. 'I wouldn't put anything past him.'

'Carl might be a lot of things but this is in another league altogether.'

Mennan and Officer Zarif have another Turkish exchange of words, making me feel even more helpless at being unable to speak the language.

'Why would Jay be trying to get Carl into trouble?' Lance asks. 'If that's what it is. What the hell's going on?'

'I wish I knew,' I reply. I feel like I've aged a hundred years in the past couple of days.

'How well do you know Carl Webb?' Mennan asks. 'No matter what you think he may or may not be capable of, the police do need to follow this accusation up. Jay isn't the only person to have mentioned him.'

'He was my boyfriend – he isn't anymore, but we've been messaging again.' Lance shoots me a look. Like it really matters who I've been texting with in the scheme of things.

'According to what we've been told, Carl Webb is *not* in England,' she tells us. 'He's here, in Bodrum.'

'But that's impossible,' I reply. 'We were only messaging last night. He said something along the lines of *I wish I were there and able to support you.*' I daren't look at Lance. After all the aggro that took place between Carl and me last year, he's well within his rights to be annoyed. I won't tell him that we actually *spoke* on the phone yesterday. 'But there is one thing—'

Everyone looks at me.

'Carl and Mum have been messaging – I saw something on her lock screen when I found her clothes yesterday.'

'Why the hell didn't you say?' Lance swings around to face me.

'I guess I pushed it to the back of my mind – I've been too

focused on *Mum* and the police finding Jay. And I thought Carl was at home.'

'What do you know about their messages?' Mennan asks.

'It was just one message and it cut off before I could read much, but there *was* some sort of threat between them. I asked Carl last night and he says he's been chasing some money my dad owed him before he died.'

If Carl really *is* in Bodrum, could he be involved? Oh my God – surely not?

'I think you've got some explaining to do, sis,' mutters Lance.

'You need to check the messages on Mum's phone,' I continue. 'I couldn't get into it.'

Mennan and Officer Zafar speak for a few moments, then he points at my bag.

'The police need *your* phone for analysis as well as your mother's,' Mennan tells me. 'Just for a couple of days. We need to look at any messages between you and Carl Webb.'

'You can't take my phone. How am I supposed to keep in touch with the hospital.'

'Hasn't your brother got one?' She nods at Lance.

'Yes, but—' Oh, I don't know why I'm bothering to argue. I reach into my bag and with shaking hands remove the lock code from my phone before handing it over. 'I'll help you in any way I can – of course I will.'

'The police now need to find Carl Webb,' she replies. 'If there's any way you can help them, you need to let us know.'

'Well if you've got her phone, she can't let you know if he messages again,' says Lance.

I nod. 'I still think Jay's lying about Carl. He wouldn't hurt Mum – he's no real reason to. She didn't approve of him, but for him to have arranged for her accident wouldn't have even crossed his mind.'

'I have to say, I'm with her on this,' Lance says. 'Carl's a pillock but not a murderer. My money's on Jay.'

'And as for my being abducted,' I continue. 'There's just no way he'd have—' We all look up as the door opens, this time with one of the nurses who originally shooed us into this room now standing there. She says something to Mennan whose face I watch for a reaction. We've been here before. This is the moment when it could all fall apart.

'You can go in and see your mother for a few minutes,' Mennan finally says, nodding towards the door. 'She's doing much better.'

I want to weep with relief as we both rush to the door.

'If we could just take your number, Lance, to keep in touch with you both.' Mennan says something to Officer Zafir who tugs a notebook and pen from his pocket. Lance turns back and gives her the info she needs before hurrying to the nurse's station after me.

Then arm in arm, my brother and I follow the nurse across the corridor to see our mum. I've got so many questions swirling around my head but still no chance of getting any answers.

30

HAYLEY

'Well, that's one weight off our mind.' Lance and I exchange the air-conditioned hospital for the heat which slaps us in the face as we exit into the late May afternoon. 'She's just resting until they slowly wake her up.'

'And she's responsive now, you heard what they said about her pupils.'

'And she squeezed my hand.' Tears fill my eyes at the memory of it. 'Three times.' I glug at the ice-cold water we've just got from the vending machine. I've never been more grateful for a cold drink.

'And mine.' Lance is never one to be outdone.

'I don't think there's going to be any lasting damage,' I say. 'She can clearly understand us.'

'Let's hope so,' Lance replies. 'But in the meantime, I'm starving.'

I laugh, for the first time today. 'That makes a refreshing change. Come on then, we'll find a place to eat and work out what we're going to do next.'

Mum might have turned a corner since we first got to the hospital this morning but my appetite hasn't. As I pick at my salad with one hand, I use Lance's phone to message Carl with the other. At least I can log in to Messenger so Carl won't have a clue that I'm not on my own phone. Somehow, I've got to find out if there are any grains of truth in what the police have been told about him. I also need to find out where he is so I can let them know.

'Have you got logged in alright?'

I nod.

'It's best if you make out she's still at death's door when you message him.' Lance stuffs the rest of his sandwich into his mouth.

'Why?'

'Why do you think? If he's involved in any way, he should be told as little as possible.'

'You're right – of course you are. I think we have a plan of sorts. We just need to piece everything together.'

'We will.' Lance lifts his second sandwich from his plate. 'I don't think the police are trying hard enough. But *we* will. Carl doesn't know I'm here, does he?'

'No,' I reply. 'I don't think I mentioned it. Right, let me send this message.'

> Sorry for only just messaging. It's all been hell. xx

The three dots to signal he's replying appear almost straight away. This means nothing yet. I'm still totally convinced that Jay's just thrown the first name he's thought of into the ring to take the heat from himself. However, if there's even a slither of a chance of *Carl* being involved in any way, then I have to find out how he's involved – and why.

> I've been worried about you, Hayles. How's your Mum doing? xx

Lance pulls a face as I show him the message. 'He can't bloody stand Mum. He's definitely up to something. And why are you putting kisses at the end of your texts?'

'To soften him.' I smile. 'And yeah, there was no love lost between them, that's for sure. He's only showing concern to try and win me over.' I return my attention to the screen.

> She's taken a turn for the worse. When I got there this morning, the crash team had just been rushed in. It was awful. xx

> How is she now? xx

> Totally out of it. She's in intensive care and I've been sent away to have a break. xx

> Will she be alright? Have they said? xx

> I don't know. But I've never felt more alone in all my life. xx

> I wish there was something I could do. xxxx

> I just wish you were here. I'd give anything for you to be here. xxx

> Do you mean that? xxxx

> Of course I do. I wouldn't have been back in touch with you for all this time if I didn't. Surely that must count for something? xxx

> What if I told you I could get to you? xxxx

> Really? You'd do that for me? xxx

> I'd do anything for you. xxx

How soon? xx

I'm actually already here. As soon as I heard, I jumped on a plane. To be around if you needed me. xxx

Oh my God! He's admitted he's here. I punch the table, making Lance jump and a few of the other diners turn to stare at us.

'Never.' He plucks the phone from my hand, shaking his head as he scans down the conversation. 'You need to find out where he's staying. I knew he was a wrong un, I just knew it.'

'This still doesn't mean Carl was behind what happened to me *or* mum, but I have to admit, it's all looking pretty dodgy.' I take the phone back from him.

So where are you staying? xx

Not far from you. xxx

'Oh my God. He knows where my hotel is.' I flash the phone screen at Lance again.

'Well, he's already shown how brilliant he is at stalking you.'

I can meet you. xxx

Lance swaps to my side of the table so he can watch over my shoulder. 'No, I don't like the sound of that. Say you'll go to wherever he's staying instead. Then we can let the police know.'

Why don't I come to you? Let me know where you are. xx

> I could do with getting out for a beer. I bet you could too. I've got nothing in the apartment. xx

'What shall I do?'

'OK – arrange to meet him. We can make sure the police are there to lift him when he arrives.'

'But what if he sees them *first* on his way in. No, to be honest, I want to eyeball him and find out what he's got to say face to face before he talks to the police. I'll know if he's lying.'

'You really don't believe he's involved, do you?'

'Not directly. But it wouldn't surprise me if he knows something.'

'You've always been a poor judge of character, Hayles, but fine, I'll be close by, watching over you and ready to call the police. And you *must* find out where he's staying.'

> You still there? xxx

Yeah, sorry, was just taking another call from the hospital. If you tell me where you are, I'll meet you, say at six o clock. xx

> Is everything OK? xxx

I'll know more soon. Where will you be? xx

> There's a bar by the harbour – The English Bar. Easy to remember. xxx

OK see you then.

'You've forgotten to add kisses,' Lance says.

31

HAYLEY

'Is it along here where the police found Jay?' Lance points across the street at the long row of bustling bars where staff are scurrying around between the tables. My attention's immediately drawn to a large dog cooling itself off in the sea in front of some of the diners, reminding me of the first night in Bodrum when Mum and I went for a meal. It seems like such a long time ago now.

In all the beach bars, the sun loungers by day are swapped to dining tables at night. The businesses must make a fortune so it's no wonder Jay's buying into one. With *our* money. We'll get to the bottom of all this – we've just got to be careful.

'Wait – look.' I follow Lance's gaze to where Jay emerges from the bar at the end and then heads towards the harbour.

'Let's get after him.'

We follow, on the other side of the road, weaving in and out of other pedestrians as Jay makes his way past a row of docked boats. Eventually, he pauses at one and cuts through the throng of people who are passing either way.

I cup my palms around my eyes, blinded by the sun.

'He's going in there.' Lance nudges me.

'This must be the boat he's living on,' I shout above the bustle of the crowd we're surrounded by.

'We should go over while he's on his own,' Lance tugs at my arm.

'That's if he is. And what would we say to him anyway?' I look at my brother like he'll have all the answers. Really, the two of us are way out of our depth. We've told the police that Jay dumped Mum and ran off with all her money, but as we were told, this doesn't prove that it's *him* who hurt her and is responsible for where she is. And what motive would Jay have to have come after *me* the other night? Perhaps Carl would have more motive for that, who knows? Nothing's making any sense at all.

'Come on, sis.'

'It's far too dodgy to go over.' Fear's snaking up my spine. 'We don't even know if he's on his own.'

'But we need to get *something* from him.' Lance isn't taking his eyes from the entrance to the boat. 'Some kind of information. The police have let him go, for God's sake.'

'I'd prefer to wait to find out what Mum remembers. It's far safer.'

'But we've no idea how long that could take.' Lance looks thoughtful. 'Look, we could just ask Jay about Carl – see what he's got to say – they're clearly in contact with one another and he's bound to trip up somewhere.'

'You're forgetting that he ran off with all Mum's money,' I say. 'He'll just want to see the back of the lot of us, especially me and you.'

'He's *bound* to say something incriminating to prove his involvement,' Lance goes on. 'Something we can record on my phone for instance.'

'I don't know if that would stand up.' Lance is forgetting what I do for a living. 'A person's consent is needed for a voice recording to be admissible in court.'

But that's in England. Maybe things are different in Turkey. I'm certainly inclined to think that *whatever* we get from either of them can only help to take things forward. The police have already let Jay go and will do the same with Carl, even after I've led them to him.

'You're being defeatest, Hayles.'

'I'm not. OK, right, we'll go over. If anything kicks off at least there's two of us.'

'I reckon he'll be pretty shocked when we turn up in front of him. That'll put him on the back foot to begin with, won't it?'

We weave through the crowd and step gingerly onto the deck of the Bodrum Belle. I go right, Lance goes left and we hide around each corner of its entrance. Peering in through the window at the side of the door, I can see Jay. He looks to be wearing swimming trunks as he enters a room to the right of the boat, slamming a door behind him.

I steady my breath before trying the door handle with my elbow. It's unlocked. I glance across at my brother before slowly depressing the handle completely and pushing the door open. If I walk away now, I'll regret it – I know I will. So, sensing my brother's presence right behind me, I tiptoe further into the boat. My gaze immediately falls on a row of keys hanging near the door. What a stupid place for a key rack – right next to an unlocked entrance door. *Main door, storage, cabin, main room, sauna, steam room.*

The smell of the sauna is the next thing I notice as we venture further forward. Jay's voice drifts from behind the door.

'That's bloody stupid. Talk about blurring the lines.'

The lack of a reply means he must be speaking on the phone. I turn to look at Lance. He pats the pocket of his shorts and nods in confirmation that he's recording like he said he would. He needs to get as close as possible to have any chance of clearly picking up Jay's voice. My heart is beating ten to the dozen as we shuffle closer. If he says something to incriminate himself, recording the conversation from out here is far preferable to confronting him.

'As I said before, neither Debra nor Hayley had *any* idea who was behind her getting chucked into that van.'

So Jay *was* involved. My heart's beating even faster now. If he catches me out here, who knows what he'll do to me? Lance is as close as he can get. I can barely get my breaths in as Jay continues talking. He's always liked the sound of his own voice so it's fairly loud. As long as he doesn't get a sense that anyone's out here. Thank God he's in a sauna that doesn't have a window.

'You couldn't even get that right, could you? It was supposed to be her bloody mother you got hold of.'

I don't believe this. So *that's* why those men suddenly dumped me from that van unhurt in the middle of the night. They didn't realise they'd snatched the wrong person – me, instead of Mum. But what's *she* ever done to hurt anyone? And who the hell is Jay speaking to? Could it be Carl?

'I don't care. I just want her out of the picture once and for all. She can take me down in so many ways – especially if it comes out about who *really* lit that match on New Year's Day.'

I stifle a gasp as Lance and I look at each other in horror. This is all messed up. Why was it reported that Dad set the fire to trap Jay if it was really the other way around? I lift a finger to my lips just in case Lance is having any thoughts about taking matters into his own hands and confronting Jay.

'No you haven't, Debra's still bloody alive isn't she? Knowing our luck, she'll pull through as well.'

I clutch onto Lance's arm. This is really, really serious – not to mention, dangerous. Anything could happen to us if we get caught out here.

'No there's no money – not a penny – not yet. Listen to me,' – His voice hardens, – 'I've built a good life for myself and Chantelle in this place – I'm not having that bitch scupper things for me, do you hear?'

'You chose the side you're on.' He's shouting now. 'So bloody stick to it.'

'I don't give a shit,' Jay yells again, 'All I'll say is that if she shows *any* sign of coming out of her coma – well, you know what you have to do. And in the meantime, if the police come around asking you anything, you keep me well out of it, have you got that?'

'You've only ever been in it for the money. I just wanted rid of *her*. Coming round here with her threats – harassing me.'

I tiptoe back towards the entrance door, Jay's words fading slightly as I get further away from the sauna.

'What are you doing?' Lance hisses as he comes after me. 'He's still talking. We need to get all this.'

'Stop the recording.' I point at his pocket. 'And I might need you to delete it, depending on what happens next.'

'What are you on about? What are you doing?'

The recording no longer matters. But what I'm about to do, really does. I cast my eyes over the row of key hooks. Ah, there it is – *sauna*. I raise my finger to my lips again and while fear sparks from Lance's eyes, he does nothing to stop me. He must know that he won't be able to.

He waits by the door as I creep back to the sauna, clutching the large metal key, and retaking my place against the wall next to the door. Jay's still talking, even more animatedly than before.

'There's more at stake here than you know. The job needs finishing.'

What he means by that needs no explanation so it's now up to Lance and me to ensure that nothing else can happen to either Mum or to *us*. I shuffle the last couple of metres to the door to have a good look at it. I can't see any hinges which must mean they're on the inside. Good. That means the door will only open inwards, making it harder for him to escape. I just need to get this key into the lock without being heard.

I'm trembling as I inch the key towards it, taking care not to touch anything where I might leave fingerprints behind.

'Of course I bloody know that.' I have to stop myself from jumping as he suddenly bellows. 'Do you think I'm stupid or something?'

Quick as a flash, I slide the key in whilst he's shouting and twist it until the door is locked. Then, covering my hand with my cardigan, I reach for the temperature dial above the door and turn it to two hundred and ten degrees fahrenheit, as high as it will go. Finally, I dart back to where I came from, giving the key handle a good wipe on my clothes as I go. In less than three seconds, I've re-hooked the key and I'm at the door which Lance is holding open with his shoulder.

'Let's get out of here,' I whisper. 'Don't touch *anything*.'

Gently, he closes the door after us and we begin walking away from the boat as nonchalantly as we can. Life out here continues. Throngs of people dodging around each other, selfies being taken against the harbour backdrop while restaurateurs try to steer passers-by into their establishments.

'Look innocent,' Lance says. 'Whatever you do, don't start running. Let's get back across the road to where we were before. There are so many people around that no one's taking any notice of us anyway.'

Standing amongst the crowd on the other side of the road, we don't speak to each other for what must be around ten minutes as we stare back over at the boat. By the time Jay decides he wants to get out of the sauna, he'll be so tired and hot that he'll quickly run out of energy when he tries to fight his way out. It seems he was too busy shouting at whoever he had on the phone to have heard the clunk of the door lock as I turned the key.

And it's so noisy out here, what with the crowds and the traffic, that even if he were to bang and shout, no one would ever hear him. He could call for help on his phone but at the heat I've turned that sauna up to, he'll have such little time to be rescued in, he might as well not bother.

32

HAYLEY

'HAYLEY, what the hell have you done?' Lance strides after me as I march along the edge of the road on the outside of everyone. I'm sick of saying, 'Excuse me' as I weave in and out of people who walk along like they haven't got a care in the world. I've been a nice girl all my life and where has it got me? Precisely nowhere. 'What if he can't get out of there?' Lance adds.

'That's the idea,' I reply. 'Come on. I need a drink and I need one right now.'

'You're joking, surely? You won't be able to live with yourself if he dies in there.'

'Watch me.' I spin around to face my brother. Fear sparks from his eyes but I've never felt more determined. I quite like this new version of myself. *Hard as nails Hayles* instead of the people-pleasing version I've come to despise. The one that was just like my mother used to be.

'He'll have an emergency stop button inside anyway.' Lance's voice relaxes. We were cut out of the same piece of cloth, my brother and I, with consciences the size of a planet. Well, not any more. After the acrimonious split with Carl last year, Dad's death and now everything that's happened to us since we arrived in Turkey, I've realised that having a conscience no longer serves me.

'There won't be *an emergency button* in that cheap and nasty sauna.' I jerk my head back towards the boat. 'It's a DIY set up – it doesn't even have a proper door.'

'We need to go back.' Lance follows my gaze. 'It's not too late to put this right. I can't stand the man any more than you can but we need to let him out of that sauna and let the police deal with him.'

'You heard what he was saying, didn't you? About Dad? And about me and Mum? What he's done to *our* family. He doesn't deserve to carry on with his swanning around. Even hell's too good for him.'

'You're better than this,' Lance reaches for my arm as I set off walking again. 'Hayles, you couldn't live any more than I could with someone's death on your conscience. Not even Jay's.'

I glance around to see if anyone's heard him. But of course, they haven't. Hardly anyone speaks much English. The hotelier says more people come over from England when the holiday season fully starts but for now, we're likely to be in the minority.

I continue striding along, the English pub on the corner where I'm meeting Carl now coming into view. I haven't been in a pub since ours burned to the ground – I haven't been able to face it.

'Jay killed our dad, Lance.' Clearly, my brother needs it all to be spelt out, before he does or says something we'll both regret. 'He's also tried to kill our mum. *And,* he was behind me getting abducted. He deserves to be roasted to death in there. I hope it's absolute agony for him.'

I turn back again – the boat's still in sight through the crowd of people. But there's been no sign of anyone coming in or out.

I wish I could ask Lance for his phone and Google, *how long could someone survive in a sauna at two hundred and ten degrees?*

But I'd better not.

It's a relief to swap the stifling hot air for the air conditioning again. If only Lance and I could just remain in here and get pissed together for the rest of the night – pretend none of it's happening. But Carl has to be faced next. And we need to get back to Mum.

After what I've just done, I can hardly believe life's going on as normal for everyone else. People are standing at the bar with no idea they've got a murderer in their midst. After all, that's what I could be. Jay might have lost consciousness by now – or perhaps be dead. Even if he took a bottle of water into the sauna, I can't imagine *anyone* could cope with being unable to escape from heat of that intensity. More than double the normal body temperature. And he'll have been in there for around twenty minutes since we left the boat. If I *ever* feel an attack of guilt in the future, all I'll have to do is remember what Jay said.

If it ever comes out who really lit that match on New Year's Day.

'Here you go, sis.' Lance pushes a large glass of wine in front of me. It's quieter in here than the other bars but then I guess it would be, being that the place prides itself on being so authentically English, but a far cry from our homely pub with its open fire and family atmosphere. I lived there my whole life and have mourned the place along with the loss of my father. It's been horrendous and that *bastard* is going to pay for what he's done to us.

'Cheers, bro.' If Mum was with us, she'd chuckle at the large gulp I take from the glass. But I've never needed a drink more.

'Are you alright, Hayley. You've gone really pale.' Lance's eyebrows knit together in concern the way Dad's used to. Sometimes, I can hardly bear to look at him. His expressions and mannerisms are so much like our father's were.

My heart's banging against my ribcage as it all begins to sink in. 'Oh my God, I can't believe what I've gone and done, Lance.' My anxiety levels are suddenly skyrocketing. I really didn't think any of it through and couldn't get past what I'd heard Jay say back there. I can't put my finger on what's bothering me the most right now – that I could be personally responsible for someone's death or whether it's just the possibility of getting caught and punished.

'I *did* try to warn you.' He's always been an *I told you so*, my brother.

'I can't exactly go back there and unlock the door, can I? Besides, he could be dead by now.'

'I wish we could know what's going on over there.' Lance lets a long breath out as he glances towards the door. 'And who he was on the phone to. Maybe someone's turned up at the boat and let him out. Or perhaps he's got out by himself. It might all be fine, you know.' He rests his hand on my arm.

'How can it be *fine*? What if I get caught, Lance? I could get thrown into a Turkish jail after what I've done. It'll be like that Midnight Express film Dad used to love. Do they have the death penalty here?' Oh my God. I really *didn't* think any of it through.

'You're gonna have to calm down, sis. People are looking at us.'

Not that anyone would suspect me, a demure, a word Dad used to use about me, five-foot-five young woman. I don't look capable of locking some big bloke in a sauna. But Lance does. And that's what's also worrying me.

'Are you sure there weren't any cameras around the boat?' My gaze falls on the camera above the bar in here. But it seems to be trained on the shops and bars rather than on the table we're sitting at. 'Did you double-check?'

'Yeah. There are a few up this way but there was *nothing* around the boats.' He looks towards the door and then back at me. 'I think it's best if I stay right here with you when *he* arrives.' As always, he can't bear to say Carl's name. 'There's a really good chance it was *him* Jay was speaking to.'

'No – you go and sit over there.' I gesture to the other side of the pub. 'Go into one of the booths.'

'But what if—'

'Look, Carl's much more likely to divulge something if I'm alone.'

'I can't believe you're even meeting him. We should just get back to Mum.'

'I've got to try this. For the sake of appearances if nothing else. At least if the police ask Carl anything about me, he'll be able to say that he met me for a drink this afternoon and that I seemed perfectly normal.'

'You're anything *but* normal right now.'

I tilt my watch towards my face. 'Well I've still got a few minutes to get myself back together, haven't I?'

'What if something kicks off? With Carl, I mean?'

'If I need you, I'll lift my bag from my feet and put it in my lap, OK?' I point down at it. 'Anyway...' I'm getting more and more antsy by the second and what I just said is true. I really *do* need to get myself back together before Carl turns up.

At the sound of it ringing, Lance tugs his phone from his pocket. 'It says *no number*.'

'Well answer it then. It could be the hospital.'

'I'll put it on speakerphone. Hello?'

'Lance Ford?'

'Yes, that's me?'

'I from American Hospital. Your mother – she wake. She ask for you and sister.'

'Oh my God, that's wonderful news.' For a split second, all the angst about what I might have done to Jay flies out of the window.

'Is she going to be alright?' Lance asks.

'Doctor speak when you here.'

'We'll be there soon.'

'She just needs another scan first so around two hours from now.'

Lance hangs up and we look at each other. 'Thank God for that,' he says. 'Finally, some good news.'

'I know, but listen. You really should go over to one of the booths now, and stay out of sight. Carl could be here at any minute. Let me deal with him and then we can focus on Mum.' I'm talking as though I haven't just locked a man in the hope of cremating him alive inside a sauna. And I'm capable of doing something similar to Carl if I discover he's been involved.

'I'm going. I'm going.' He snatches up his bottle of beer and marches off to the other side of the bar. Clearly I've upset him. Yes, I'd love to celebrate that mum's turned a huge corner but first – Carl.

We're just in time for no sooner has Lance disappeared into the booth that Carl suddenly appears in the doorway. And he has a look on his face that I really can't decipher.

33

HAYLEY

'HAYLEY.' He strides towards me, his biceps rippling beneath the sleeves of his Lacoste T-shirt. I bet he's bought that since he's been here at Turkish prices – he was never able to afford designer gear back home. His eyes look bluer in his sunburned face and I hate myself for making such an observation. He definitely looks to have been here longer than he's letting on. He points to my empty glass. 'Another?'

His demeanor is impossible to read at this first glance but no matter what, I'll get to the bottom of things. If he knows *anything*, I'll get it out of him.

'Oh, that glass was already here,' I fib. When we were together, I wasn't a big drinker and I don't want him getting suspicious. 'But I'll have a white wine if you're offering.' I might as well get another one down me. My nerves are shot.

My eyes must bore holes into Carl's back as he waits at the bar. I notice movement from Lance's booth and can see the top of his head poking around it. True to his word, he's not taking his eyes off me.

'It's not like you to arrive early.' Carl rests the glass in front of me. 'Remember when we were dating? You were always late.' His eyes crinkle in the corners as he smiles. He's clearly pleased to see me. Perhaps this *is* his only agenda, after all. I'm really praying he's not involved.

He does look good. Far better than I remember. Maybe he *has* seen the light since we split last year. The tone of his texts has certainly changed. They went from abrupt when we were together to almost sinister after we'd split up. When *he* didn't want me, but equally, he didn't want anyone else to have me. But now, the tone of his texts has become attentive and caring. And like he's always happy to hear from me.

'Thanks.' I reach for the glass.

'It's great to see you,' he says. 'You seem to be bearing up well, considering.'

What I need to do is to lull him into a false sense of security before I catch him on the back foot with my questions. 'It's lovely to see you too.'

'Is it *really*?' His smile broadens. Perhaps I shouldn't have said that. I need to be careful here.

'Of course. After what's happened...' My voice trails off. I *can't* let him know that Mum's rallied and that her recovery is now a good possibility. He still needs to believe she's still at death's door. If there's even a grain of truth in Jay's accusations, whoever was responsible for Mum's 'accident,' might try to finish what they started. And Mum couldn't possibly undergo any more injury. It will still be a miracle if she returns *completely* to normal after what she's been through.

'Has there been any more news on your mum since we were texting before?'

His expression looks to me like *feigned* concern. And I could be wrong but it seems like he's trying too hard to keep his voice nonchalant. Carl knows more than he's planning to let on – I'm certain of it. But I'll play along.

'Not a thing, unfortunately. I'm going back in a couple of hours. But in the meantime, it's good to get a break from the place. Gosh, I need this.' I take a large slurp from my wine. It makes a change for Carl to buy me a drink. Usually, it was me buying them for him, or, when we had the pub, sneaking him pints from behind the bar. My insides sag at the memory. I'd give anything for things to be back to where they were and to be able to have Dad back.

'Do you know any more about it all?' He runs his fingers down his bottle, wiping the condensation away. He isn't letting the subject go, that's for certain. 'How she ended up like she did, I mean?'

OK, so he's asked the question. Therefore I'll have to return it to him. It's now or never and this, after all, is the main reason I've agreed to meet him. To be able to eyeball him as I wait for his answers. 'That's what I want to ask *you* about actually?'

'What do you mean?' His face tightens, reminding me of the *old* Carl. The one I came to fear. 'Ask me about *what?*'

'Well. for some reason, the police have asked me if I know you.' I might as well just come out with it. We're in a public place and I'm safe. Lance is over there, keeping an eye on me. Carl will be able to put another spin on the one-sided conversation I heard Jay involved in before. Before I did what I did. My heart twists at the recollection of what I've become responsible for.

'The *police* have?' His voice rises. 'But where could they have got *my* name from?'

'You tell me.'

'You sound like you're accusing me of something, Hayles.' His frown deepens. 'When I've only been in Turkey since this morning.' He swigs from his bottle. 'Is *this* the only reason you agreed to meet me?' His voice has taken on a sharp edge. 'To see what you could get out of me. And there was me thinking—'

'Look Carl.' I'm not taking my eyes off his face. 'I'm really hoping I can trust you. Which is why I'm here in the first place.' No matter what, I've got to keep him on my side. I'm going to need him to vouch for me and the fact I couldn't have anything to do with what's happened to Jay. By the time he's found in that sauna, no one will know *exactly* how long he's been in there, after all.

'What exactly did the police say to you?' Carl seems to have paled beneath his sunburn as he awaits my reply. Oh God, I desperately *don't* want him to have had anything to do with it all.

'Jay's told them you're involved in some stuff.'

'*Jay* has?' His voice is louder this time and there's definitely a trace of anger within it. 'As in your former bar manager?'

'He's not my former *anything*. Not after how he treated my mother. He took everything she had and just dumped her.'

'What's he said about me? What *stuff*? I've got to be honest, Hayley – I haven't even seen the man since last year.'

'So why's he told them that you're' – I point at him – 'responsible for me getting thrown into the back of a van the other night?'

'What van? What are you talking about? And how could I have been? I wasn't even here *the other night*?'

'Well, that's what he's told them. He's given them your name so they're looking for *you*.'

'As if I'd do something like that.' Carl looks hurt. 'I know I didn't show it when I had the chance, but you were the most important person in my world. I was even hoping...' His voice trails off. 'Oh God, the police aren't *believing* what he says, are they?'

'I don't know,' I reply. 'But they definitely want to speak to you – if only to rule you out.'

'Well thanks for the warning.'

It's on the tip of my tongue to say, *It wasn't supposed to be a warning.* Instead I say, 'But that's not all.'

'Go on.' He slurps from his bottle as though he needs the alcohol as much as I do. It's not every day you're told the police are after you – especially in a foreign country.

'He's also told them that *you're* behind what happened to Mum. That *you* did it.' I'm watching him more carefully than I ever have.

He chokes on his beer. I wait for a moment while he recovers himself. This is why I've met him in person. I needed to see his reactions to these questions for myself and right now, I'm becoming more convinced that Jay could be wholly responsible. Especially after what I heard him saying in that sauna. But who he was on the phone to is still a mystery.

However, what I can't lose sight of is that the two of them *must* be in contact on some level, for Jay to have known Carl was in Turkey and to have thrown his name into the ring.

'Am I to assume that if you believed any of this crap for one moment, you wouldn't even be sitting here?' He's wide-eyed as he waits for my reply. 'Whose side are you on, Hayles?'

'My mother's, as it happens. But I want to know why Jay's been saying these things about you.'

'So do I?' He grits his teeth as he shakes his head.

'I didn't even realise you had anything much to do with each other.'

'We don't.' He takes a deep breath and keeps his eye fixed on the table, avoiding my gaze. I'm getting a sense that he's seriously deliberating whether to be honest with me. 'Not really.'

'Go on.'

'The truth is that Jay got in contact with *me*. Yesterday, as it happens.'

'Why?'

'He wanted to know if I was still in touch with you and whether I could do anything to help *call off the dogs* as he put it, meaning your mother.'

'*Call off the dogs*. She was only trying to get her money back from him. She had every right to pursue him.'

'He offered to pay me to help him.'

I wish I could trust what Carl's saying here but he's got that shake in his voice as he always has when he's lying.

'*Help*, in what way? At least I know now what you're *really* doing here.' As if I could have believed he'd jumped on a plane to support *me*. I'm such an idiot. *Gullible*, as Dad would say.

'No! It *is* like I told you. I couldn't bear for you to be on your own over here. You've got to know what I still think of you.'

'OK so *suppose* you're telling me the truth?' I draw air quotes around the word *suppose*. 'Why the hell would Jay lie to the police? Why's he blaming *you* for everything?'

'Because he *knows* I'm here now. He rang me again when I was at the airport. But I promise you – he's trying to stitch me up.'

I'm beginning to feel even more justified for trapping Jay in that sauna. Just terrified that I'll be caught.

'How do I know I can trust you?'

'Because you *know* me, Hayles.' He gives me a look I remember only too well. I've seen it before and he was lying *then*. Perhaps he's forgetting just how well I do know him.

But there can be no denying that he reminds me of the Carl from our early days together. I take another gulp from my glass as I try to chase the thought from my mind. It's not serving me one iota.

'Can I ask you something else?'

'Ask away.' He leans back in his chair and clasps his hands behind his head. It still feels surreal that I'm sitting at this table with him, here in Bodrum. He can tell me until he's blue in the face that he's flown here on a whim, merely to support me. But I'm not buying it at all. On some level, he and Jay have been in league together. Jay offering him some money speaks volumes. Carl's never turned down a money-making opportunity.

'What *work* did you do for my dad? What did he owe you money for.'

'Oh, this and that.' He waves his hand but I won't be dismissed so easily.

'Which means nothing to me. Come on, Carl. Dad was a sparky. And you barely know a plug from a lightbulb.'

'I was helping him with the business side of things if you must know. Drumming up trade, accounts, that sort of thing.'

'Five grands worth of work?' I shake my head.

'There was tons more besides. Work I did on his website, his social media, other marketing.'

'So where is it all then? How come we've never seen any of this *work*?'

'Cos none of it had chance to go live before he—.' He looks sheepish. Whether it's because he's stopped himself saying the word *died*, or whether it's because he's lying through his teeth is anyone's guess.

'Since when have you been the techy type? And why did Dad never mention any of this to us?'

'Gosh, you've drunk that quickly.' He points at my glass.

'You're changing the subject.'

'Do you want another?'

'Just a small one then.' I'm feeling the effects of the alcohol. But while I've drunk enough to calm me down a little, if I drink much more, I'll be neither use nor ornament by the time we get to Mum.

I'm getting nowhere here though. Carl, as always, seems to have an answer for everything.

The wail of passing sirens strikes fear into my core.

'What's the matter?' Carl sets a glass in front of me as he follows my gaze to the door. 'It's only an ambulance, Hayles. Oh, two ambulances.' More vehicles screech by. 'And three police cars.' He cranes his neck.

Why *two* ambulances? Why an ambulance at all? If they're heading to that boat, ambulances *could* mean that Jay's still alive.

34

HAYLEY

I'VE FLED to the toilets. I need to get myself back together. I can't think straight, I can't even breathe properly. Oh my God, I can't work out how I feel - I both want Jay to be dead and *don't* want him to be. I've never felt more mixed up in my life.

'Are you alright?' Carl asks as I retake my seat.

'I, um. I guess their noise just brought things back to me. The other day, I mean. With my mum.' I stare into my drink as there's an extended beep of a horn. It sounds crazy out there.

'It's bound to bring things back.' Carl reaches over the table and cups his hand over mine, tugging it sharply away as the shadow of my brother looms over us.

'What's going on here?' Lance demands, anger sparking from his eyes as he looks from Carl to me. 'You're supposed to be getting to the bottom of things, Hayley, not having a cosy second drink together.'

'Where did *you* spring from?' He and Carl stare at each other. 'You never said he–'

'I could ask *you* the same question, Carl.'

'I've already explained myself to Hayley. I don't owe *you* any explanation.'

'I knew this was a bad idea,' Lance says. The sharp edge in his voice makes him sound like Dad again as he looks from Carl and then back to me. 'How can you even sit here with a man the police are looking for in connection with what happened not only to Mum but to *you* as well?'

'He says it wasn't him. He's saying—'

'And how can you believe a word that comes out of his mouth? Are you mad?'

'I'm off to pay a visit.' Carl nods in the direction of the toilets. 'I'll leave the two of you to scrap it out. If you'd told me your brother was going to turn up, Hayles, I'd have left things alone with you.'

I watch as he retreats. 'There was no need to storm over all guns blazing, was there?'

'There was *every* need. It's been making my blood boil, watching you. Well – was it worth it?'

'I don't think he's got anything to do with me *or* Mum, bro. Like I said before, he's capable of many things, but abduction and attempted mur—'

'Hang on a sec.' Lance frowns at me and jerks his head in the direction of the men who've just sat down at the table behind us. 'Just for a minute.'

'Why?'

'Shush.'

'Yeah,' One of them says, obviously as English as Lance and I are. 'Didn't you hear the bloke in the ciggy shop – he was talking to one of the ambulance drivers who told him they've got two bodies in there. A bloke and they reckon the other one is his wife or girlfriend.'

'How the hell do you manage to get yourself trapped in a sauna?' The other man says. 'That's what I don't understand.'

'*Two bodies?*' I mouth the words at Lance who looks just as shocked as I am.

I didn't hear a *second* voice in there. Shit. Shit. Shit. What the hell have I done? The thought of taking one life feels dreadful enough, no matter how justified – but *two*? So who the hell is it?

'I can't imagine it was a pleasant way to go,' the man says, glancing at the door as another siren shrieks by. 'Roasting to death like that.'

Why all the sirens? If they're already dead, I want to ask Lance but I don't want to miss any of this conversation.

'Heatstroke? I agree. They rang for help but it was so hot in there, the services didn't have a chance of making it in time.'

'Carl's coming back,' Lance hisses. 'Act normal. And don't say another word.'

I'd love to witness Carl's reaction to the news that his so-called friend, or whatever he is to him, is dead – that could be interesting. But I imagine it will take a while for Jay to be formally identified and named.

So, I've *killed* two people. Me, Hayley Ford, who's never so much as swatted a spider or acquired a speeding ticket, has ended someone's life. I'm a murderer. The thing is, after what Jay's done to our family, I'd do it to him all over again. But not his girlfriend, if that's who it was. That's going to be a more difficult burden for me to live with, assuming I even get away with this.

Carl retakes his seat opposite me and looks at Lance as if he's the biggest imposition he's ever encountered.

'We're going to get back to the hospital,' I tell Carl, sliding my drink across the table to Lance. 'You finish it.'

I've achieved as much as I can here. I should have my alibi, and I'm certain that while Carl isn't telling me the full story, he isn't capable of what Jay was trying to pin on him.

'Don't mind if I do.' Lance knocks it back in two large gulps. 'Come on then, Mum'll be expecting us to be there when they've finished her scan.'

Carl's head jerks up. 'Hang on, I thought you said she was *completely* out of it?'

'Erm, yes, well, but erm, we've still been told she can hear us.' I'm stuttering and Lance has coloured up.

'Why are you lying to me, Hayles?'

'*Hayles.*' Lance glares at him. 'What's going on with you two?'

'Nothing at all,' I reply. 'Look, alright, I fibbed about Mum when you first arrived. We're still worried someone will try and get to her. But I'm sorry I lied.'

'It's OK.' He looks hurt. 'You must have realised now that you can trust me.'

'I'll drop you a text later.'

'What the hell are you playing at?' Lance literally drags me along as we head back in the same direction we arrived from, back past Jay's boat.

'Says you, big mouth! He wasn't supposed to know Mum's come round.'

'Haven't you learned your lesson where Carl's concerned? What makes you think you can trust him all of a sudden?'

'Which question shall I answer first.' I could almost laugh if there was anything to laugh at. 'Jay's the only person who's been a danger to any of us. And I think I *do* trust Carl. He hot-footed it onto a plane when he thought I was on my own, dealing with Mum. He cares about me.'

'So you're getting back together then?'

'I can't even think along those lines right now. Oh no—' I stop dead in my tracks. It feels like my heart might stop as well.

'Oh my God.' Lance stiffens and tightens his grip on my arm.

An aisle has parted through the crowd of onlookers and a body bag is being lifted through it.

'What the hell have I done?' My jaw drops as straight after the first one, a second body bag is brought out and placed into the same vehicle as the first. I've killed two people. I'm nothing but a murderer. I choke back a sob.

'Keep it together, sis,' Lance hisses into my ear as he tugs me onto the road away from the crowd. 'No one's got a clue we have anything to do with this. Let's get to the hotel and we can talk about it there.'

'I just want to get to Mum. If they end up arresting me I need to see her first.'

'Keep your bloody voice down. No one's going to arrest you. What you need to do is to sober up.'

'I'm perfectly sober.'

'No you're not. Let's just get past this lot.'

'I can live with myself with what I've done to Jay.' I can't take my eyes off the van containing the bodies. 'But not the other—.'

'Come on, sis – let's just keep moving.' Lance tugs at me. 'With our pasty bodies and English accents we stick out like sore thumbs already.'

The wine I drank is churning in my stomach as we make our way past the private ambulances and flashing lights of the police presence that's gathered along the harbour. 'I think I'm going to be sick.' I clutch at my belly.

'Don't you dare.' Lance continues to guide me along. 'Let's get back to the hotel so you can pull yourself together and we'll get a taxi to Mum from there.'

The police look to have pushed everyone back to our side of the road and I take deep breaths as we fight our way through the crowd. Lance is right – I can't be sick here. Talk about drawing attention to myself.

'Keep moving.' Lance's hand rests between my shoulder blades. 'Come on, sis. I've got you.'

35

TINA

'Mum – it's me.'

'Where the hell are you? I've been here all afternoon, waiting like you told me to.' The truth is that I've been climbing the walls especially with not knowing what's going on one way or another. And with no money to spend, what else was I supposed to do anyway? There's only so much window shopping and aimless wandering around that someone can do.

'I've been allowed to make one phone call.'

My breath catches. 'What do you mean, *allowed to make one phone call*?'

'I'm at Bodrum Police Station. I've been arrested.'

'*Arrested*? You're joking. What the hell for?' Like I really need to ask.

'On suspicion of murder, abduction, attempted murder, the lot. There was a policeman jabbering away in Turkish and then an interpreter repeating everything he said.' Carl's voice is echoey and sounds far away. 'Mum, you've got to help me.'

'Oh my God, but, but, what the hell have they got on you?' This isn't happening. Never in my wildest nightmares when all this began did I think my son would be arrested.

'I don't know.' Carl's voice is almost a whimper. Oh my God, *anything* could happen to him. He's in a foreign jail. They could even have the death penalty here for all I know. 'They've rung someone for me – someone from the British Embassy, but I'll need you to get me a lawyer too.'

'But, we haven't any money to pay a lawyer with.'

Think, think, Tina. What the hell am I going to do?

'We'll have to find a way, Mum.'

'OK, let me make some phone calls. But no, wait, first we need to see what they say to you from the Embassy. *They* might even sort a lawyer for you. How long did they say it would take?'

'I've only just been brought in. Oh Mum, I can't believe it. They're going to photograph me and all that before they lock me up and then I've just got to wait.'

'Where were you anyway? What happened? How come they came after *you*?'

'I met Hayley.' There's a load of clanking and banging in the background and for a moment, I think I've misheard him.

'*Hayley!* After everything we—'

'Hayley told me Jay had pointed the finger at me for Debra's accident – I guess that's why they arrested me. She was having a break from the intensive care ward – Debra's on the mend so she felt able to leave her.'

Debra's on the mend. So casually mentioned.

'And then what?'

'Something must have happened at the harbour as there were suddenly police and ambulances all over the place. Anyway, I followed Hayley and her brother after we'd parted company but just as they went into their hotel, a load of police suddenly came out of nowhere and wrestled me to the ground.'

A voice sounds in the background.

'I think they're telling me to hurry, Mum.'

'You need to find out what they could have on you.'

'They haven't told me much.'

'Don't answer any questions until you've spoken to the Embassy.'

'I won't.'

'Try and stay calm. We'll get you out of there. We'll get this sorted—'

One way or another. But he doesn't hear my last sentence. Whoever was telling him to hurry seems to have cut him off.

I'm not sure what I'd do without Google Translate. I've written everything I'll need on scraps of paper in the taxi, starting with the Turkish for Intensive Care so I can follow the signs. Then I've got some notes that should ensure I'll be let in to see her.

I'm a close friend of Debra Ford's, my note reads in Turkish. *I've travelled from England to be with her.*

In case the nurses need any further persuasion, my second note says, *I've promised her children I'll sit with her.*

If Hayley and her brother have managed to get there before me, I'll just turn around and walk away. I know exactly what *she* looks like – just like her mother. But neither of them should have a clue who I am. Hayley might have seen me fleetingly at her father's funeral but she didn't look to be paying close attention. Which is what happens when you get to my age – you just fade into the background.

My heart hammers in my chest as I approach the ward. I press the buzzer. 'Debra Ford,' I stammer as it's answered.

Something's rattled off to me in Turkish. Eventually, the door's opened and a nurse stands before me. I show her my note. She looks confused as she takes it from me and disappears inside again.

Oh bloody hell. I drum my fingers against the wall as I try to steady my breathing. A minute passes, then another, then another. Where is that nurse? I've got to get into Debra's room before anyone else shows up. I know Hayley and Lance were back at their hotel before but they could easily be on their way here by now. Which is why I've decided to prioritise this visit before finding some help for Carl.

Finally, the door opens and the nurse returns my note to me with six words scribbled beneath it.

ara yoğun bakım ünitesi.ara ünite

She then points at a sign with the same words.

'Thank you.' I strike my hand against my heart as I've seen several Turkish people do when they're grateful for something, and then set off in the direction of wherever Debra's been moved to.

I'm trying to put the knowledge that my son's being held in a Turkish police station to the back of my mind. I'm here for one reason only – after all, we've got little else left to lose.

Eventually, after several wrong turns, I reach where I'm supposed to be, and get through the door just as someone's coming out of it. My heart's thudding as I stride as confidently as I can towards the nurse's station. I give the nurse who's sitting there my most nonchalant smile as I show her the words in Turkish explaining who I am and who I'm here to see. So far, so good.

She looks me up and down and frowns so I pass her the other to say I've promised Debra's children that I'll sit with her. Eventually a smile of sorts crosses her lips and she points me in the direction of what looks like a side room.

Get *her*. Debra's even ended up with her own side room. Her sort always come up smelling of roses. Really, she should be heading to be buried six feet beneath them.

I smile back at the nurse again as I take a deep breath and step forward.

The door to Debra's room's ajar and her light's dimmed. She's wired up to several monitors but they're not going to get in my way. Literally or physically. I'm here for one reason and one reason only.

'Hello, Debra.' I pull the blind down over the window in her door as I close it gently behind me.

Her eyes widen as she grapples about for what looks like the remote control that's been left at her side on the bed. Quick as a flash, I'm across the room and plucking it from her fingers. Her mouth forms a terrified O.

'You're quite the sight for sore eyes, aren't you Debra?'

She's trying to sit up. I push her back.

'In fact, you look like you've done a couple of rounds with a speedboat.' I laugh as I perch beside her on the bed. She tries to jerk away from me but winces with what must be the pain. I shove myself up closer to her, glancing at the door just to double-check the nurse hasn't decided to follow me in. I can't imagine anyone will bother us for a few minutes. After all, I'm just in here keeping my friend company after her ordeal.

'What do you want?' Her voice is raspy. She must have had the tubes stuck down her throat. She'll have more than them stuck down her throat by the time I've finished with her.

'I must admit, you've done pretty well to still be here. Especially after how you looked when I left you.'

She tries again to sit up and I push her back down by the shoulder and she yelps. 'Shut up,' I hiss. 'Because of *you* and your family, my son's been locked up. But we're going to get him out of there and then we're going to get away from here.'

'Please, just go.' Her lips are dry and cracked. She's a shadow of the confident, assured woman I met only a few months ago. After all that's happened, she'll have learned a hard lesson. However, I'm here to finish what I started and I can't let her appearance dissuade me.

'Jay's paying me to do a job – he went to all the trouble of hiring a speedboat for me, only I didn't manage to get it right the first time, did I? So I'm just here to finish things off.' When he first suggested the speedboat, I baulked at the idea. But driving it was easy once I'd got used to it, the hardest part of what he wanted me to do was keeping her under surveillance and waiting for my opportunity. When they'd discussed travelling together, she'd told Jay about her plans for early morning swims in the sea. It was my job to ensure this was her final one but I failed miserably. I won't fail again.

'Please. No more.' The same terror glows from her as when we locked eyes as she was swimming in the sea. Once again, the power's all mine, but this time, I'm going to end things properly. I'll see her through to the very final moment before quietly slipping out again. Her face is in such a mess already that no one will suspect anyone's made it worse since when they do their post mortem.

Finally, we'll get the money we've been promised. No one in Turkey, apart from Jay, has a clue who I am and by the time anyone starts trying to work it out, I'll be back on a plane to England. The police can't possibly have anything much on Carl – after all, he had nothing to do with any of it. They'll have to let him go.

'I'll pay you. Whatever you want?'

'I thought you had no money.' I snarl into her face. 'You and your stuck-up family – all looking down your noses at the likes of me and Carl. I'm sick of being the one who has nothing, the one who's always overlooked and left until last. While people like *you*' – I prod my finger into her chest and she yelps again, louder this time – 'trample all over us.'

'You crazy bitch.'

She cries out when I yank one of the pillows from behind her head and it falls back. I need to do what I came here for and get out. One minute's all it will take. 'I'll show you who's a crazy bitch, shall I?'

'No.' I muffle her voice beneath the pillow as I slam it over her face and begin to press down, praying that nobody out there will have heard her voice.

She wriggles beneath me, her arms and legs thrashing as she attempts to fight me off. However, in the state she's in, she surely knows as well as I do that she doesn't stand a chance.

Still, she's putting up more of a fight than I expected. I force *all* my weight onto the pillow.

Just a few more seconds and she'll be dead.

36

DEBRA

'IF WE'RE GOING DOWN, you're coming with us.'

My neck cracks with the extra weight as Tina forces the pillow down even harder over my face. I close my eyes against the pain – it feels like something might explode yet I'm powerless to defend myself.

The faces of my kids enter my head as the energy to fight subsides, along with my breath. She's getting the better of me and I'm going to meet my violent death, here, alone with this monster of a woman – someone I thought was a friend. Perhaps this is all I deserve and Bryn will no doubt be the first thing I see after death to tell me so.

Somewhere in the corridor, an alarm fires up, perhaps the last thing I'm ever going to hear, while that woman's face will also be the last thing I'll see. There's a bang, an angry shout, then suddenly, the pillow's ripped away from my face as Lance hurls Tina to the ground. 'Get help, Hayles,' he cries.

'Mum, oh Mum.' He cradles my head in his hands. 'Breathe, come on, you're safe, we're here now. She can't hurt you anymore.'

I gasp into the face of my son as the alarm continues to wail.

Someone else out there must be in trouble. But it'll be nothing compared to what we've had in here.

Then as Lance jerks his head back up again and my vision starts to clear, I spot the glint of metal. I can't get any words out but I try to point as Hayley shrieks, 'She's got a knife.'

Tina lurches back towards me so Hayley leaps forward and onto Tina's back, attempting to separate her from the knife by grabbing her wrist. I've always taught my children that if a knife's involved, always give them whatever they want, no matter what the cost. I never dreamed it would be *my* life that would hang in the balance. Hayley screeches as Tina slashes the back of her arm and drops back to the floor, blood dripping through her hands.

'Please,' I croak. I want to say, *kill me, but please, don't hurt my daughter.* However the words won't form themselves. I continue to wheeze as I try to get my breath back after being without oxygen for so long. A few more seconds and I'd have passed out. A few more seconds still and it would have been all over.

Lance is yelling for help but seemingly can't make himself heard above the alarm. Nor can he get to the door as Tina slams Hayley up against it, blocking his path.

'Let her go.' Lance springs from beside me to where Tina's pressed Hayley against the door and is holding the knife to the side of her neck. 'Oh my God, please – look, just stop. I don't know who you are or what you want but—'

'Aren't you going to introduce us, Debra?' There's a flash of yellowing teeth as she grins in my direction.

'Help,' I call out but my voice is so feeble, it's almost laughable. Under normal circumstances, I'd be across that room and protecting my daughter, but I can't move. Where the hell are the staff? Why can't they hear what's going on? How did she even get in?

'Lance,' Hayley sobs as she stretches her arm around the side of Tina towards him. I want to tell her to keep calm and to keep still but I still can't get enough breath in.

'Stay where you are,' Tina snarls at Lance, momentarily waving the knife in his direction before returning the point of the blade to Hayley's neck. I don't know what's turned Tina so badly but she's totally lost it. 'As for you, you little bitch.' Hayley cries out as she grabs a fistful of her hair and wrenches her head back. 'You might have my *son* where you want him with all your little games but we both know what you *really* think of him, don't we?'

'You're *Carl's* mum? Oh my God. Oww.' Tina must tug harder at Hayley's hair at the sound of her voice. I try to sit up again but the intensity of the pain in my head and my chest forces me back. That woman could do *anything* to my daughter and I'm powerless to stop her. In the absence of anyone coming to help, it's all down to Lance.

I point at the call bell which Tina snatched from me when she first barged in here. Lance edges towards it. I try to meet his eye, needing to convey *slow down* to him. All it takes is one wrong move and it could be all over.

'Get back,' Tina bellows at him. But I don't think she's realised he's going after the call bell.

'Help!' Hayley's voice is weak.

Lance stops in his tracks. "What is it you want from us? Why are you doing this to my sister?'

'She wants money,' I gasp. 'Just give her whatever we've got. She – she's the one – when I was swimming.'

'Please, just let me go,' cries Hayley. 'You can have as much as you want.'

'Her *dead.*' Tina spins around and points the knife in my direction, gritting her teeth. Oh my God, she's going to come at *me* again. I brace myself.

'Somebody, help.'

Lance kicks the knife, karate-style out of her hand, sending it spinning across the floor. As Tina drops to her knees to retrieve it, the door bursts open, also sending Hayley sprawling.

'Her, it's her.' I point at Tina. 'She's got a blade.' The security guard looks confused as he follows my gaze to where Tina's on all fours, her hand over the handle of the knife. She's close enough where in one move she could rise from the floor, lurch in my direction and plunge it into me. After all, I'm powerless to go anywhere. Hayley and Lance are thankfully, just out of her reach.

'Let me out of here.' She points the knife at the officer as she rises to her knees.

There's a shout from the doorway in Turkish as another two security guards appear. As one of them heads towards her, she raises the knife and jabs it in his direction.

He shouts something in Turkish to the other who darts to the far side of Tina as she tries to slash this way and that with the knife. Between them they quickly manage to restrain her arm, releasing the knife from her grip as they pin her face down to the floor. She continues to squirm around as the third officer kicks the knife further out of the way.

'You're safe now, Mum.' Lance grabs my hand between the two of his.

Hayley crashes onto the floor at the side of the bed and rests her head onto her hands, sobbing. 'Come here,' I lift my arm. 'As Lance just said, you're safe now. It's over.'

'I wish I could have some of that stuff and fall asleep with you.' Hayley watches as my painkiller's topped up. She hasn't stopped crying since Tina was handcuffed and dragged away by the police.

They've got Carl in custody too and I can't believe what that family's been capable of. I want to say this out loud but I'm just too tired to speak any more.

'The main thing is that we've survived.' Lance's voice is fading as my painkiller takes hold. 'And we'll soon be able to go back home and put all this behind us.'

I can no longer keep my eyes open and drift back into the safety of sleep.

I'm still here, my children are safe and we're all together. With each of their hands in mine, my daughter's sobs and Lance's voice softly ebb away.

EPILOGUE

DEBRA

'A VERY WARM welcome on board this morning's flight with British Airways.'

It's wonderful to hear an English accent again. Since Hayley and Lance left for England just over a week ago, I've been stuck with Google Translate and hand gestures to make myself understood. Lance had to get back to university for his assessments, and because Jennefer was taking her kids away for half term, Hayley had to get back to look after Sammy. I stretch my leg out, grateful for the extra room to accomodate my plastered foot.

'This is the 14:02 flight to Leeds Bradford and after we've finished refuelling, we'll be preparing for departure. We're blessed with a tailwind as we follow our flight path over Europe and can expect to land back in Leeds at a little before four o'clock local time. The weather in Leeds is a little drizzly, and be warned, the temperatures there are somewhat cooler than what you'll have become accustomed to here in Bodrum – you've got the balmy heights of fourteen degrees ready to greet you.'

'Great,' the woman next to me mutters. 'As if we're going home to *that*.'

'Well, I for one, can't wait to get back,' I reply. I surprised the kids this morning when I told them I was being discharged. It had been expected that I'd be in hospital for at least another week and one of them was going to fly back and accompany me home. 'I've been in hospital for over three weeks.'

'Yes, you've clearly been in the wars.' She twists in her seat as if to take a better look – sling, stiches, pots and all. 'I hope whatever it was happened towards the *end* of your holiday and that you were able to enjoy some of it.'

'It's a long story,' I reply, hoping my tone conveys that it's not one I want to tell right now. 'But at least it's behind me.'

'I hope you had good medical insurance.' She hasn't phrased it as a question but it feels like one.

'Yes, thankfully. And my friends at home had a whip round to cover all the extras.' This is the understatement of the century. Hayley and I cried on the phone together when she returned home last week and discovered what the former punters of The Dales Inn had raised through a JustGiving page they'd set up. I don't deserve it in the slightest but it's wonderful to know how much they all must think of me.

'I'm Jayne.' She offers her hand. 'Since we'll be sitting together for the next four hours, we may as well be on first-name terms.'

'Debra.' I accept her handshake. 'And I'll be glad of some company when the G&T trolley comes around.' I can't help but be struck by the irony of my words. After all, look what has happened since the last time I shared a G&T with a fellow passenger while journeying home.

I settle back into my seat as the plane takes off. I can't wait to be back with Hayley, Lance and Sammy, a privilege I was so nearly robbed of. I'll never, ever take it for granted again.

'So did you have a nice break?' I turn back to Jayne as the plane soars higher. I hate this part of the take off process so welcome the distraction of conversation. The possibility of pleasant small talk is far preferable to spending the next four hours alone with my thoughts. I've had far too much thinking time, driving myself mad in the hospital as it is.

'Lovely, thank you. But it's such a shame about those other English people – the man and his girlfriend.' She shakes her head. 'Did you hear about it? Found dead in a sauna? What a dreadful business. There's only one way they'll be flying home.'

'Yes, I heard.' I do my best to keep my voice steady. Jayne doesn't need to know anything in depth about me. 'The woman responsible is lucky she's being flown back to the UK to stand trial and be sentenced, rather than seeing her time out in Turkey.'

Tina won't be seeing daylight for a *very* long time. That is, apart from when she's allowed out in the prison yard for exercise. She's facing charges for two counts of murder against Jay and Chantelle, two counts of attempted murder against me, aiding and abetting an abduction *and* making threats with a weapon. She admitted to the last charge, after all, she was caught with the knife but she's trying to wriggle out of the rest of it. Thank God for Lance kicking the knife from her hand like he did – at least all those karate lessons he had as a boy have paid off.

The nightmares I was having of Bryn grabbing me by the throat have been replaced with the pillow being forced down onto my face but I'm sure, in time, they'll fade away.

'Her son was eventually freed without charge, wasn't he? It was all a very strange business.'

I nod. Bloody Carl. Hayley's told me she's finally blocked him and will ignore any attempts he makes to contact her in the future. She's known him a long time and has *always* had a weakness where he's concerned. However, she seems to have realised that she's far better off without him. It's better to be alone than with someone who's so wrong on every level.

I thought I couldn't stand to be alone but with everything that's happened, I've found that I'm actually looking forward to embracing this next chapter of my life – being self-sufficient and answering to nobody but myself. It's taken a lot of soul searching to get here but no way will I ever dance to anyone else's tune again.

There's a beep, the seatbelt sign disappears and Jayne unclips hers. 'Ah, that's better, we can relax now. So have you been on holiday on your own?' She glances towards my left hand, evidently looking for a wedding ring. I'll never be wearing one of those again.

'I'm widowed actually.' I glance from the window at the fluffy white clouds. I always love the view from the aeroplane window. Brilliant blue sky against what looks like snow. I'm so lucky to be able to see it again.

'Oh, I'm sorry,' she replies. 'Is it a recent bereavement?'

'Do you mind if we talk about something else?' I feel for the finger where my rings used to be. 'Sorry, I'm not being rude – it's just that so much has happened recently and I'm trying to look to the future now – rather than lingering in the past.'

'Of course.' She smiles as the air hostess pauses beside our row of seats with the trolley. 'I think we're both having a G&T, aren't we, Debra?'

We continue to chat as our drinks are fixed for us.

'Cheers.' We touch plastic cups and she adds, 'to the future.'

'To the future,' I repeat, trying to swallow the lump in my throat and the tears stabbing at the backs of my eyes. I so nearly didn't have one.

'So you're a fellow Yorkshire lass?' Jayne says. 'I dare say you've got even more of an accent than I have.'

'Not so much of a lass anymore,' I reply with a chuckle. 'It's not so long since I turned fifty.'

'It's a good age.' Jayne nods knowingly. 'When you're wise enough to know better but old enough not to give a rat's arse about what anyone thinks.'

'I'll drink to that.' I raise my drink into the air before placing it in the cup holder and touching the scar on the side of my head. 'Getting older is a privilege denied to so many, isn't it?'

It was very nearly denied to me.

I don't deserve to be here after what happened to Bryn. My vision was not only clouded by my ridiculous feelings for Jay, but also by vanity and the chasing of my lost youth.

By some miracle, my kids don't know anything of the truth so it's a guilty secret that I'll be able to carry to my grave. But I'll spend the rest of my life doing whatever I can to atone. It's taken a lot to change me, to make me realise what's important.

And it's a lesson I'll never lose.

Before you go...

Thank you for reading Last One Standing, the sequel to Last Orders – I hope you enjoyed it!

If you want more, check out The Valentine on Amazon, my next psychological thriller, where you'll meet Tamara, who's looking forward to a Valentine's Day with her fiance, Dale at a secluded location. However, a sinister case of mistaken identity means their 'celebrations' may not turn out as perfectly as she'd intended...

And for a FREE novella, please Join my 'keep in touch' list where I can also keep you posted of special offers and new releases. You can join by visiting my website www.mariafrankland.co.uk.

BOOK CLUB DISCUSSION QUESTIONS

1. Discuss the theme of justice in respect of the main characters who it applies to - Debra, Hayley, Jay, Carl and Tina. To what extent did each of them receive justice - or not?

2. Who, in your opinion, was the biggest victim in this story?

3. How have the characters changed since book 1, Last Orders?

4. To what degree did the Turkish setting play a role in the story?

5. How might each of the characters go on from here?

6. What message does the book leave you with?

7. Money is the root of all evil. Discuss this well-known phrase in connection to this book.

8. To what extent did greed influence each of the character's behaviours?

9. Was Hayley right to let her guard down with Carl? Has he deserved any forgiveness?

10. Discuss how the theme of ageing manifested itself in the story?

11. How did Lance and Hayley support one another?

12. How much doubt has been cast in their minds about their

mother? If they were to discover the truth about her past actions, would she deserve their forgiveness?

THE VALENTINE – PROLOGUE

Blue swirling lights cut through the mist as we get nearer to the pin on the map.

'What the hell's going on?' It's a rhetorical question – one that neither of us can possibly know the answer to but I know what the saying *blood runs cold* means. It's literally happening to me.

We get as close as we can, abandoning the car where crime scene tape has been stretched across the lane. Too far to see who's in there for myself but close enough to glimpse the chocolate box house, and...

the body bag that's being carried out.

We look at each other in horror. I dart forwards – I've every right to. 'Oh my God – what's going on?'

'Stand back.'

'But that could be my—'

'This is a crime scene.' An officer catches my arm and tugs me back. 'Stay back here.'

'Please tell me what's going on. I think I know the...' My voice trails off as he cuts in.

'Formal identification will take place in the next few hours,' he replies, his hand remaining on my arm. 'If you could just let us get on with our jobs.'

'But...'

'Leave your number with me.' He pulls a notepad from his pocket. 'I'll get the commanding officer to contact you when we've finished up here.' His tone tells me this isn't up for discussion.

The body's laid in the back of a private ambulance as I continue to watch on.

'You could at least tell me if it's a man or a woman in there.'

'I can't tell you anything. Not yet.'

Find out more on Amazon

INTERVIEW WITH THE AUTHOR

Q: Where do your ideas come from?

A: I'm no stranger to turbulent times, and these provide lots of raw material. People, places, situations, experiences – they're all great novel fodder!

Q: Why do you write psychological thrillers?

A: I'm intrigued why people can be most at risk from someone who should love them. Novels are a safe place to explore the worst of toxic relationships.

Q: Does that mean you're a dark person?

A: We thriller writers pour our darkness into stories, so we're the nicest people you could meet – it's those romance writers you should watch...

Q: What do readers say?

A: That I write gripping stories with unexpected twists, about people you could know and situations that could happen to anyone. So beware...

Q: What's the best thing about being a writer?

A: You lovely readers. I read all my reviews, and answer all emails and social media comments. Hearing from readers absolutely makes my day, whether it's via email or through social media.

Q: Who are you and where are you from?

A: A born 'n' bred Yorkshire lass, I've recently passed the ripe old age of 50, which wasn't as painful as I'd feared! I have two grown up sons and a Sproodle called Molly. (Springer/Poodle!) My 40's were the best: I've done an MA in Creative Writing, made writing my full time job, and found the happy-ever-after that doesn't exist in my writing - after marrying for the second time just before the pandemic.

Q: Do you have a newsletter I could join?

A: I certainly do. Go to www.mariafrankland.co.uk or click here through your eBook to join my awesome community of readers. When you do, I'll send you a free novella – 'The Brother in Law.'

ACKNOWLEDGMENTS

Thank you, as always, to my amazing husband, Michael. He's my first reader, and is vital with my editing process for each of my novels. His belief in me means more than I can say.

A special acknowledgement goes to my wonderful advance reader team, who took the time and trouble to read an advance copy of Last One Standing and offer feedback. They are a vital part of my author business and I don't know what I would do without them.

I will always be grateful to Leeds Trinity University and my MA in Creative Writing Tutors there, Martyn, Amina and Oz. My Masters degree in 2015 was the springboard into being able to write as a profession.

And thanks especially, to you, the reader. Thank you for taking the time to read this story. I really hope you enjoyed it.

Printed in Great Britain
by Amazon